**"You don't have** your body."

With that, Jack swept her into his arms and delivered the kiss to end all kisses. She was so shocked initially she didn't know what to do. Longing welled up within her, unlike anything she had ever dreamed she could feel. A shiver of need swept through her, followed by an even more magnificent ripple of pure pleasure.

Even while her mind protested, the rest of her—heart, body and soul—surrendered to the sweet surprise of his kiss. And the knowledge that maybe, just maybe, she had really misread this man in thinking that he had no heart.

She leaned closer, emboldened by the ferocity of her response, wanting, needing to know and experience more....

And just that suddenly, he released her.

Looking down at her with a distinctly male satisfaction, he surveyed her lazily from head to toe. "Still think I haven't got a romantic bone in my body?"

Dear Reader,

Spring is the season of renewal. And what better way to add new energy and excitement to your life than by falling in love and making a lifelong commitment to another person?

At least that's the way Jack Gaines's long-widowed mother feels. Sixtysomething Patrice is engaged to be married. Jack would be happy for her if he believed his mother was truly in love with Dutch.

But something seems missing in their relationship. And Jack, burned by his own matrimonial "mistake," does not want to see his mother enter into an ill-advised union. She's had enough heartbreak in her life. As her son, it is his duty to protect her.

Enter Caroline Mayer, wedding planner extraordinaire. Although Caroline has ruled out a happy-ever-after romance for herself, she loves fulfilling the dreams of others by making their wedding the happiest day of all.

Caroline and Jack are at odds from the beginning. He wants to stop the wedding. She wants the nuptials to go off without a hitch. What they don't expect is to fall in love themselves along the way....

I hope you all enjoy winter's end and experience a little spring fever and a lot of love. In the meantime...

Happy reading,

*Cathy Gillen Thacker*

# Cathy Gillen Thacker
## WANTED: ONE MOMMY

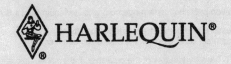

HARLEQUIN®

TORONTO • NEW YORK • LONDON
AMSTERDAM • PARIS • SYDNEY • HAMBURG
STOCKHOLM • ATHENS • TOKYO • MILAN • MADRID
PRAGUE • WARSAW • BUDAPEST • AUCKLAND

Recycling programs
for this product may
not exist in your area.

ISBN-13: 978-0-373-75302-4

WANTED: ONE MOMMY

**Printed in U.S.A.**

# ABOUT THE AUTHOR

Cathy Gillen Thacker is married and a mother of three. She and her husband spent eighteen years in Texas and now reside in North Carolina. Her mysteries, romantic comedies and heartwarming family stories have made numerous appearances on bestseller lists, but her best reward, she says, is knowing one of her books made someone's day a little brighter. A popular Harlequin author for many years, she loves telling passionate stories with happy endings, and thinks nothing beats a good romance and a hot cup of tea! You can visit Cathy's Web site at www.cathygillenthacker.com for more information on her upcoming and previously published books, recipes and a list of her favorite things.

## Books by Cathy Gillen Thacker

# Chapter One

"I want you to stop the wedding." Caroline Mayer knew there was going to be trouble when the bride's son insisted on meeting with her in advance of her consultation with the "happy couple." But she wasn't prepared for the CEO's blunt demand.

She stared up at Jack Gaines. Caroline had no doubt that the thirty-four-year-old owner of Gaines Communication Systems was used to getting exactly what he wanted. Most men that handsome, wealthy and successful were. But the implacable Texan had targeted the wrong person to put a halt to the nuptials of his equally wealthy and successful mother.

Aside from the fact what he was asking her to do was just plain wrong, the Gaines–Ambrose nuptials could make or break her. If she failed to deliver the most talked about wedding of the year, her career as a bridal consultant would be over, almost before it began. If she succeeded, she would be the new hot wedding planner in Fort Worth. With that would come long-lasting financial security and the realization of all her dreams. She'd be able to buy a home, adopt a child, get a dog, continue to expand her business and save for the future.

Caroline flashed Jack Gaines a droll smile. She wanted him to know with whom he was dealing. "Obviously there's been a miscommunication." She paused to let her words sink in. "I'm a wedding planner. Not a spoilsport for hire."

And that was a shame, Caroline thought. Because although she wasn't looking to get involved with anyone just now—or maybe ever—she was still a woman who appreciated beauty in all forms, and Jack Gaines was a man who was very easy on the eyes.

Every inch of him, from the top of his clipped dark brown hair and chiseled masculine features, to the toes of his custom leather boots, was perfectly and precisely cared for. His face was clean shaven, his jaw solid, his lips kissable. His powerful six-foot-two frame boasted broad shoulders, an impossibly solid chest and a trim waist. But it was his expressive, silver-gray eyes that really drew her in. This was a man who missed nothing, a confident indomitable male, the kind of man who let nothing stand in his way. The kind she had sworn off, with very good reason, for the rest of her life....

Jack moved to impede any hope of a dignified exit and challenged her with a glance. "Hear me out."

Caroline shifted the heavy weight of her monogrammed briefcase to both hands and held it in front of her knees. Simmering with a resentment she had no idea how to handle, she held his gaze deliberately and said, "I don't think that's going to be necessary. The answer to you is no." She still planned to say yes to his mother and her fiancé.

He studied her, a thoughtful expression on his handsome face. "Even if doing so would save my mother from a public grief and humiliation she doesn't expect and surely doesn't deserve?"

Caroline set her briefcase down. Maybe she could do someone a favor here—although it wouldn't be Jack

Gaines. "What makes you so sure your mother is going to be hurt?"

Jack's eyes darkened. "She barely knows Dutch Ambrose."

But plenty of people knew of Dutch, Caroline argued silently. His string of rental properties on South Padre Island was the most sought after vacation venue in the area. Unfortunately, they were out of Caroline's price range—for now, anyway—but that hadn't kept her from admiring the glossy photos of the luxurious beach houses in the promotional brochures available in every grocery store in the state. "Patrice must think otherwise, or she wouldn't have agreed to marry him."

His expression adamant, Jack folded his arms across his chest. "He's rushing her into this."

Somehow, Caroline doubted that. Struggling to ignore her reaction to his nearness, she stepped back slightly. "The Patrice Gaines I've read about in the Fort Worth newspapers is not a woman to be rushed into anything."

Jack twisted his lips into a skeptical line.

Annoyed by his attitude, she went on. "I mean, how many years did your mom hold on to her perfume formula before finally selling out to that big cosmetics company?"

Jack shook his head and scoffed. "Thirty. But that's not the point."

Caroline held up a palm, silencing him. "It's *exactly* the point. Your mother knows her own mind. And if she wants to marry Dutch Ambrose, then she should—with no interference from you!"

He narrowed his gaze at her. "You're saying you won't help me."

She was going to have to let this job go. Better to steer clear of it than find herself in the middle of a familial contretemps that could ruin an otherwise spectacular wedding day, and along with it, her hard-earned professional reputation.

Her thoughts turned to the memory of another handsome, determined male, and the heartache he'd caused her while claiming to have *her* best interests at heart. What was it with guys, anyway, that made them think they knew better than the women in their lives, and hence, needed to go all out to protect them?

"Even if I pay you a lot of money?" Jack persisted.

Those words brought Caroline back to the present. She had nothing against the quest for money. She was doing everything she could to make a better, more secure life for herself, too, and like it or not, that meant having money in the bank. But the assumption that she could be bought rankled. She absolutely would not do to someone else what had been done to her. And it was time Jack Gaines found that out!

Caroline propped her hands on her hips and glared at him, making no effort to disguise her contempt. "Let's get something clear, Mr. Gaines. I will not help you betray your mother. I will not destroy her dreams. And I most definitely will not smile and say one thing to her face and then go behind her back and do something else that will break her heart and simultaneously benefit me. And furthermore, I'm insulted that you would even ask!"

With that, Caroline picked up her briefcase and stalked out.

"WHAT DO YOU MEAN Caroline Mayer refused to plan my wedding?" Patrice Gaines demanded later that same day as she looked up from the notepad in her hand. A veteran list maker, Patrice was rarely without paper and pen.

Jack cast a glance at his seven-year-old daughter, Maddie, out in the yard, throwing a ball for her accident-prone dog, Bounder. Relieved that at the moment the sweet-tempered and energetic two-year-old golden retriever was not involved in any mischief, or doing anything that would require yet another emergency trip to the vet, and that his equally lively daughter was happily entertained, caring for her favorite "friend and companion," Jack smiled. At least two members of the Gaines clan were happy.

Jack pushed aside his guilt at his deception and turned back to his mother with a shrug. "I'm sorry, Mom. I asked her this afternoon. She said no." And a lot of other things he would prefer his mother never hear.

Patrice put down her list, took off her bifocals and let them rest on the gold chain around her neck. "Caroline Mayer is the best up-and-coming wedding planner in the entire Fort Worth area! Weddings masterminded by her are incredible, memorable events!"

"So you mentioned," Jack said drily, trying not to think about the elegant woman who had shot him down and then walked off without a backward glance. It wasn't just her refusal to be intimidated by him that kept Caroline Mayer in his thoughts. Or the tousled layers of copper hair that framed her face and curved against her chin. It was the mix of innocence and cynicism in her crystal-blue eyes. The sense that she'd been around the block more than once when it came to business and having her pride hurt.

He'd heard she had not come from money, yet she was elegance defined, from her high femininely sculpted cheekbones and pert nose to the slender curves on her five-foot-five frame.

She knew how to dress—as had been evidenced by her pale pink business pantsuit, silk shell and heels. She knew what understated jewelry to wear. The only thing lacking in her presence, Jack had noted, was perfume. Caroline hadn't worn any.

Although the subtle sunny fragrance of her hair and skin had been pleasurable enough. He wondered, when she did wear perfume, what kind of scent did she favor? Something light and innocent, or mysterious and deeply sensual?

Oblivious to the direction of his thoughts, Jack's mother pressed on. "Is it money? Did you not offer her enough? Is that it?"

"We never got to the part about the money," Jack admitted reluctantly. "And I told you, if you're going to get married, I want to be the one to pay for it."

Patrice frowned. "Was there a conflict with the time frame I selected, then? Is that the problem?"

Jack thought of the ramrod set of Caroline Mayer's slender spine and the seductive sway of her hips as she stalked out. Coming or going, she was one beautiful woman—who now couldn't stand the sight of him. Jack cleared his throat. "We never got that far, either."

Clearly exasperated, Patrice threw up her hands. "Then why did she say no?"

*Because she's a wedding planner, not a spoilsport.* And I made the mistake of being honest with her about my sentiments regarding the impending nuptials, Jack thought irritably. Caroline hadn't accepted the fact he was only trying to protect his mother from a mistake that could destroy her. Aware his mother was still waiting for a plausible explanation, Jack said finally, "It was just a personality thing, Mom." *Clashing personalities.* "The woman took an instant dislike to me."

Astonishment warred with the skepticism on her face. Patrice furrowed an artfully shaped brow. "I know you can be a bit linear at times, especially when you're involved with your work…"

Why not just say it? Jack thought. *There are times when I lack people skills*….

"But surely Caroline Mayer has worked with her share of engineers and other task-specific people before. She knows how, well…unromantic…and practical to the point of insanity…you all can be."

"Thanks, Mom," Jack said wryly.

"You know what I mean. I know you sometimes say and do the wrong thing, but it's always obvious to me you mean well and have a good heart."

"Well, she apparently didn't think so," Jack muttered.

"Why on earth not?" His mother looked all the more perplexed and incensed.

Not about to go down that road, Jack shrugged and said carefully, "Bottom line—I think I just annoyed her on a lot of levels, and she decided she would rather not have to deal with me."

"I don't want anyone else," Patrice said stubbornly.

Dutch Ambrose, Patrice's fiancé, chose this time to wander into the room. On the surface, the guy was the perfect husband for his petite blonde mother. Tall, rangy, slightly stooped—at sixty-two, Dutch had a ready smile, a full head of thick white hair and the kind of deep ever-present tan that came from years spent at the beach and on the golf course. He dressed in sneakers, bright plaid golf pants, solid polo shirts and cardigan sweaters. He'd been practicing his shot in the study, and had his putter and a golf ball in hand. "What's the problem?" Dutch asked genially, as unerringly polite as ever.

Patrice looked over at the fiancé she'd only known three months, and explained the difficulty Jack had encountered with Caroline Mayer.

Jack had only to look at his mother's face to know where this was going.

"I'll call her again," Jack promised. "I'll get down on my knees and beg, if necessary."

"No," his mother said even more firmly, giving him The Look that had always preceded a grounding when he was a kid. "*You* won't."

"WHO IS HERE TO SEE ME?" Caroline asked her administrative assistant from her office in Weddings Unlimited.

Looking much younger than her fifty-something years, Sela Ramirez shut the door behind her. Her vibrant red-and-gold dress sparkled in the late-afternoon sunlight as she crossed the all-white office and stood before Caroline's sleek glass-and-chrome desk. "Jack and Patrice Gaines, a little girl named Maddie, her dog and another gentleman, Dutch Ambrose."

He was here—the take-charge man with the arresting silvery gray eyes who had already commandeered her lunch hour, and had her thinking about him off and on most of the day. Caroline pushed away from her laptop computer and sat back in her chair. "You're kidding."

Sela propped a hand on the voluptuous curve of her hip. "You only wish I was kidding."

Why did the wealthy always have to be so eccentric? Caroline wondered. *Because they could....*

"Would you like me to tell them you're too busy to see them?" Sela asked.

"No." Caroline sighed, thinking. If they were this determined, they'd find some way to see her. At least this confrontation, if that was what it was, would be private. There would be talk enough when word got out she had turned down the job, and speculation why—which, as a courtesy, she would not answer. Caroline went back to her laptop and finished updating her To Do list for the day, checking off all the items she had completed thus far. "Just give me a moment, and have them all come in. And, Sela, while they are here, hold my calls."

"Will do."

A minute later, all four of her guests trooped in. Well, Caroline amended silently, taking a moment to study her uninvited guests. Jack *strode* in, looking every bit as reluctant to be there as she was to have him. His mother, Patrice, was every bit as blonde and petite and elegant as the photos that always appeared in the paper. And she smelled incredible, as if she were wearing one of the signature scents she had been famous for before she sold her business. She was on the arm of a dapper white-haired gentleman, who also looked to be in his early sixties. A little girl who was all tomboy followed. The color of her dark brown bob matched Jack's. She wore a backward baseball cap, T-shirt and overall shorts, snow-white cotton athletic socks and dirty sneakers. She had a fluffy, and quite large, golden retriever loping at her side. Not on a leash, Caroline noted, but then, at least for the moment, the dog did not appear to need one. It looked intent on staying close to its mistress.

"We'll cut straight to the chase," Patrice said regally, after quickly and expertly making introductions. "I understand you've refused to plan my wedding to Dutch—and I want to know why!"

Jack regarded Caroline with a poker face—except for his silver-gray eyes. They were pleading for her not to give him away.

It would serve you right, she thought, if I did.

"Please help us," Dutch Ambrose said.

Maddie stopped petting her dog, long enough to look up.

"Can Bounder be in the wedding, too?" Her big blue-gray eyes danced with delight at the idea.

Caroline imagined the little tomboy walking down the aisle with a basket of flowers in her hands, the big berib-boned dog beside her, and felt a seismic shift inside her—the increasingly loud ticking of her biological clock. The familiar longing for a little girl of her own, and the deeper, more elemental need to have someone, something, in her life—beside the business she had spent the past two years building—to love.

Aware this little girl was everything she had ever imag-ined in a daughter of her own, and more, Caroline told herself to be reasonable—not romantic. And the reality was she was still running a business and needed to concentrate on that, rather than her deep-seated, private longings.

Feeling calmer, she lifted a hand and pasted on the brisk businesslike smile that had soothed many a frantic bridal party.

"We're getting ahead of ourselves here." *Boy, are we getting ahead of ourselves. Imagining what it would be like to have a child just as adorable as Maddie, as my own....*

Jack cleared his throat and broke in. "I tried explaining to Mom that it just wasn't going to work out. You and I—" he looked at Caroline with a meaning only she could read "—we're just not on the same page."

"So avoid her!" Patrice fumed, disapproving. She turned to her son and said impatiently, "I never said I wanted you involved in the planning of my wedding, anyway. You're the one who insisted on paying for it!"

"And it would be my pleasure," Jack reiterated with what seemed to be sincerity, Caroline noted. It was his turn to look distressed. "I just don't understand why the nuptials have to be this month."

This month? Caroline thought, a little shocked. April was already half over!

"When you get to be our age, you'll understand time is not something to be wasted," Dutch cut in with a wink and a grin.

Patrice smiled back at Dutch. She grasped his hand, looking up at him. "Especially with the two of us," Patrice said quietly, with a meaningful expression. She squeezed Dutch's hand once again.

Abruptly, silence fell.

Caroline, who was usually pretty attuned to these things, felt something *did* seem to be odd about this match. And that was as off-putting for her as it apparently was for Jack.

And for them to be trying to tie the knot in less than two weeks... Something was definitely strange about his. No wonder Jack was trying to stop it. He must feel something was just a little off, too.

Telling herself that it was her job to arrange weddings, not lives, Caroline cleared her throat, as well. If Patrice and Dutch wanted to marry for reasons of compatibility and companionship, as she was one day wont to do, if at all, then that was their business and no one else's.

Especially since Caroline knew better than anyone that True Love simply was not fated to happen for everyone.

Some people, like her, had one shot at big romance, if they were lucky, and if that failed...well, odds were it wouldn't happen again.

That didn't mean a person couldn't be happy and pursue other dreams, like owning their own business, or one day adopting a child who wouldn't otherwise have a home, as her mother had, and she planned to do when the time was right.

"A wedding in April is tough to arrange, even a year in advance."

"For anyone else, probably," Patrice concurred, one successful businesswoman to another. "For you? Honey, we've heard you work miracles."

CAROLINE WASN'T SURE how it happened. One minute she was standing there explaining why she couldn't take on the Gaines–Ambrose wedding, the next she was agreeing to have dinner with the family at Jack's place the following evening. They would pay her for the consult, of course, to discuss other options for the family.

To her relief, once that was set, they all left as unexpectedly as they had arrived.

As soon as the coast was clear, Sela came back in to ask with her customary frankness, "Why did you agree to that?"

There were pluses and minuses to having an assistant who was the same age her own mother would have been, who often viewed herself as the replacement to the mom Caroline had lost to illness when she was eighteen. The plus was that she had someone to act as a parent to her when she still needed one. The minus was that she sometimes found herself explaining things she would rather not have, to the veteran mother of five grown children, grandmother to eight, and full-time arbiter of love.

Caroline sighed and ran a hand through her hair. "Honestly? I don't know."

Sela studied her over the rim of the folder in her arms. "It had something to do with Jack Gaines, didn't it?"

"Of course not!" Caroline successfully fought back a flush of embarrassment.

To no avail—she still didn't fool the woman who had seen her through the tumultuous aftermath of her failed engagement and the beginning of her business. "The little girl, then," Sela persisted gently.

That assertion, Caroline noted, was a little closer to the mark. "Maddie was everything I would ever want in a daughter." And it wasn't just her short cap of dark brown hair and expressive little face, or her big blue-gray eyes with the fringe of long lashes. It was the way the little girl carried herself—with big-girl confidence. The affection she showed her dog. The liveliness in her smile.

Maddie was a ray of sunshine in an otherwise gloomy spring day. And she deserved better than a daddy who would try and derail his own mother's wedding.

Caroline didn't doubt that Jack had misgivings. They might even be warranted. But his going behind a loved one's back to try and achieve a different result than the one his loved one wanted reminded her of another man, and another time, and her own resulting heartache....

She wouldn't visit that kind of unhappiness on anyone.

Particularly a little girl caught in the cross fire of the family brouhaha sure to come if Jack stayed on this particular path.

So for that reason, and that reason most of all, she was going to do what she never did—get personally involved in a situation that was really none of her business, and see what she could do to dissuade him. And to do that, she was going to have to meet with him alone. Again.

# Chapter Two

Jack was standing on a ladder, his head in the elevator shaft, when the walkie-talkie on his belt let loose with a static string of mostly unintelligible words. "Who's here to see me?" he asked above the sound of power drills, reverberating from several floors above.

"Caroline Mayer," a cool voice said behind him.

Jack ventured a look down at the elevator floor. From his perch on the ladder he saw those crystal-blue eyes staring up at him.

Hoping she was there to make peace—not cancel on his mom and the rest of the family for that evening—Jack hooked the walkie-talkie back on his belt, set his tools on the metal shelf and climbed down the steps until they stood face-to-face. Desire caught fire inside him, throwing him off guard. "We have to stop meeting like this."

She propped her hands on her slender hips. "Ha-ha."

The pulse in her throat was throbbing much too quickly. He twisted his lips into a crooked line, then murmured offhandedly, "Glad you think I'm funny."

She made no effort to mask her pique. "What exactly were you doing?"

Jack shrugged. "What does it look like I was doing? I was taking apart a security camera that isn't functioning the way it should."

Temper flared in her cheeks, turning them a rosy coral. "Don't you have people who do this sort of thing for you?"

Yes, he had employees. Two hundred of them, in fact, most of who were at this very moment working on the computer and phone and satellite systems all over One Trinity River Place. Comprised of office space, retail stores, restaurants and luxury condominiums in the heart of downtown Fort Worth, the high-rise was a visible testament to his success and that of his four best friends. But, Jack noted, Caroline did not seem any more impressed with his achievement than she was with his efforts to protect his family.

So be it.

"That doesn't mean I can't work, too," Jack shot back, keeping his eyes on hers. "In case you hadn't noticed, I'm a hands-on type of guy."

Who was always putting his foot in his mouth, especially around her, Jack thought, noting her telltale blush of awareness at his unintended pun.

"Not that I…" He started to apologize, stopped at the ice in her eyes.

"What?" She was daring him to go on. To take the opportunity and make some sort of pass. Which he knew she would promptly reject.

Determined to come out the victor in this little battle of wills, Jack relaxed, shook his head. "Nothing."

Caroline scoffed and glanced away. As she did so, Jack noticed the pulse jumping in her throat. Was it his imagination, or was the heat of their two bodies, standing so improbably close together, making the elevator cage really warm?

Jack drew a deep breath. Once again, he noticed her

lack of perfume. And the sunny, subtle fragrance of her hair and skin.

He wondered if that was by accident or design, and what kind of fragrance she would choose when she did wear perfume. What would she wear on a date? Or to make love…

Not that he needed to know *that*. The two of them were already at an impasse and never likely to go down that road. Which was yet another reason to keep this unexpected tête-à-tête short, Jack thought.

He put a suitable amount of disinterest in his manner—the kind he had used to push away women. After his wife had left, the word had gotten out what a mistrusting cynic he had become.

"What did you need?" he asked curtly.

She looked equally ambivalent. "To warn you."

Jack's brow furrowed. He thought he had been the one calling the shots, since it was his family who had been trying to employ her services. "Oh?"

"I thought about it overnight and I've decided to plan your mother's wedding for her."

Jack bit down on an oath. He massaged the rigid muscles along the base of his neck. "Does she know?"

Caroline looked at him, nonchalant. "Not yet."

He surveyed her with exaggerated politeness. "Why are you telling me?"

Caroline's expression became inscrutable once again. "Because I also wanted you to know I wouldn't tell her what you asked me to do yesterday."

Jack wasn't sure he wanted to be beholden to her. Or any woman, for that matter. He let the lift of his brows say it all. "Why not?"

Her eyes clouded over. "I don't want to hurt Patrice."

That, Jack had to admire. Still, once you had been fooled

and abandoned the heartless way he had been, you couldn't help but be on the alert for the next scam. "So this isn't blackmail."

Caroline recoiled slightly in shock, uttered a mirthless laugh and said drily, "It hadn't occurred to me." Her blue eyes gleamed with sincerity. She waved her hand delicately. "But if you would prefer..."

What Jack would prefer was to have never made the mistake of trying to enlist Caroline Mayer's help in the first place. But since he couldn't undo that action, he figured they had no choice but to be exceedingly clear with one another. "So you're not going to help me try and put the brakes on my mother's rash decision?"

Caroline leaned closer. "Not only am I not going to help, I'm going to make sure your mother's dreams—as they pertain to her wedding—do come true."

Dread spiraled through Jack as he thought of his mother having to endure any more unexpected emotional pain than she had already suffered in this lifetime. No one had been able to do anything about the first time. Now, it was different. Now, he could take action. "And if I continue to feel otherwise and try and derail things because it's the only way I know how to protect my mother?"

"I'll find out," Caroline Mayer promised resolutely. "And I'll bust you the moment I do."

"WHOA. SOUNDS LIKE SHE put you on notice," Grady McCabe told Jack. He and his friends and fellow businessmen had met for a pickup basketball game at the local gym later that evening.

Travis Carson dribbled past, handling the ball as easily as any construction project that came his way. "Either that or the lady wants an excuse to stay close to you."

"Why would you think that?" Jack demanded in

frustration, then stole the ball and dribbled to the basket, shot, watched with satisfaction as it slid in.

"Probably..." Dan Kingsland caught the rebound and propelled the ball through the hoop, earning another two points for his "team" "...because it's clear the woman got under your skin in what...two minutes of meeting her?"

Less, Jack thought, recalling his initial visceral reaction to the woman. Dan, an architect, was pretty perceptive. There was just something about Caroline Mayer that had stopped Jack in his tracks, mesmerized, every testosterone-laced inch of him on red-hot alert. But that was probably easily explained, too, given the fact he hadn't been near a woman since his divorce from Vanessa, and could happily live the rest of his life without ever losing hold of his senses and falling in love again.

Jack argued with a frown, "It wasn't that tempestuous."

"Might as well have been, given the way you've been talking about it," Nate Hutchinson, the only bachelor in the group, said. As a successful financial advisor and all-around great guy, it was likely Nate wouldn't be single for long.

All the guys nodded their agreement. Nate caught the ball and passed it to Grady.

Jack tried to steal it before Grady could shoot, but failed. Irritably, he raced back down to the other end of the court, continuing, "The point is now Ms. Mayer's made me feel guilty about trying to stymie my mother's plans."

"As well you should." Grady guarded Jack with steely resolve.

Dan intercepted the ball meant for Jack. "Your mom is a grown woman, perfectly capable of making her own decisions," he said.

Remorse washed over Jack yet again. Damned if he'd

ignore his instincts—which told him something was definitely amiss in Dutch and his mom's plans! Jack tipped the ball out of Dan's hands before Dan could shoot.

"Furthermore—" Nate scowled as Jack's shot hit the backboard before dropping through the net "—it's not at all like you to be so devious and underhanded. It'd be one thing if you knew for certain that Dutch Ambrose was out to get your mom's money. But unless you uncover proof that something is in the wrong," Nate continued as Travis captured the ball once again, "you really do need to back off and simply be happy for them."

"And maybe," Grady finished with a provoking grin, "find something else—or someone else—to occupy your time."

CAROLINE PARKED IN FRONT of the white brick Georgian with the slate-gray roof and trim precisely at six o'clock. The two-story suburban home where Jack Gaines resided with his mother and daughter was situated on a half-acre lot in a well-established neighborhood, full of manicured lawns and towering live oak shade trees. The beds on either side of the elegant front portico, with the steeply pitched roof, sported a rainbow mix of fragrant spring flowers. The neatly trimmed bushes next to them were bursting with vibrant green leaves.

Her heartbeat accelerated with the prospect of seeing Jack again and Caroline slung her laptop bag over her shoulder, wheeling her briefcase full of demo products up to the door.

Patrice answered the door, her granddaughter, Maddie, and her dog, Bounder, right beside her. "Hi, Ms. Mayer!"

Caroline got down so she was on eye-level with the little tomboy, who today was clad in knee-length striped overalls, a child-size cowgirl hat, a navy T-shirt and round-toed brown construction boots. "Hi, Maddie. How are you today?"

"I'm fine!" Maddie beamed, bobbing around, delighted by the attention. "Do you want to say hello to Bounder? She's been waiting for you, too!"

Hearing her name, the golden retriever pranced about and wagged her tail so hard she nearly fell over. "Hello, Bounder." Caroline patted the dog's fluffy blond head. "You're a cutie." Caroline looked back at Maddie with interest. It was clear the little girl adored the dog as much as the dog adored the little girl. Together, they made a sweet pair. "How did your doggie get her name?"

"When she was a puppy, she bounded all over the place. So I called her Bounder, and my daddy and Gram said that sounded like a good name."

"It is a good name."

Bounder wagged even harder and licked Caroline's hand.

"She's kissing you!" Maddie explained in excitement. "That means Bounder loves you!"

"I can see that." Caroline gave Bounder a final pat, smiled at Maddie and stood up.

Caroline looked at Patrice, who had been watching the greetings and subsequent exchange with unbridled interest. "Where do you want to set up?" Caroline asked the bride-to-be, unable to help but think, from the pleased way Patrice was still looking at her, that she had just passed some kind of Gaines family initiation by getting along with child and dog.

Patrice smiled kindly. "The kitchen, I think. That way Jack can be a part of the discussion while he cooks."

Patrice led the way through the two-story foyer down a short hall to the rear of the home. It had clearly been built with comfort in mind. The kitchen—with its earth-toned walls, maple cabinets, granite counters and state-of-the-art stainless steel appliances—was clearly a male domain. As was the breakfast room, with its large round table and comfortable tan leather swivel chairs. The family room was beside it, where a wall of windows let light spill into a room dominated by a white stone fireplace. The opposite wall was taken up with an impressive array of built-in bookcases filled with books, CDs, DVDs and an impressive-looking plasma TV and stereo system. Along with heavy wood furniture and several comfortable plush sofas and club chairs all artfully arranged, were a collection of toys, and a big round dog bed for Bounder—who leaped up on the sofa, next to Maddie, where the two proceeded to cuddle contentedly.

Jack was dressed in a marine-blue cotton T-shirt and jeans. His dark brown hair was a little rumpled, his rugged jaw sporting a hint of evening beard. His eyes were on high alert and his lower lip curled in polite acknowledgment when he saw her.

Noting he looked very much at home, moving about the kitchen from counter to sink to stove, Caroline couldn't help but admire him. It was all she could do to follow the simplest recipe, and even those she screwed up half the time.

Aware her pulse had jumped up a notch just being in Jack's presence, Caroline set up her laptop in front of the seat designated for her, while Patrice brought a tray of crudités and ranch dip to the table.

Patrice settled next to Dutch. The two elders exchanged encouraging smiles while Caroline powered up her computer. "Okay, down to business. The first thing is the date. I've checked all the major venues and they are all booked for the last two weeks of April, but there are a few openings for the first weekend in May. The only problem with that Saturday is that it's May 5. Or Cinco de Mayo, which as you know, is the holiday that celebrates Mexico's independence from Spain, and is always a big deal here in Texas."

"Well, then that knocks out that weekend," Jack remarked, not all that unhappily, Caroline noted.

Caroline watched as he split several avocados and used the blade of the knife to pull out the seed. His culinary skill was impressive. His attitude was not. And his mother obviously agreed.

"And why is that?" Patrice asked Jack drolly.

He shrugged his broad shoulders, suggesting the answer was obvious, and sent his mother a cursory glance designed to hide his feelings. "You don't want to get married when everyone is partying."

"That's exactly when we want to get married!" Patrice said.

Dutch looked at Patrice and just smiled, as if he would go along with whatever the bride wanted.

Studying them, Caroline thought, maybe the two had a more intimate relationship than she had originally thought. Maybe Dutch and Patrice, being older than the typical bride and groom, were just shy about showing their feelings to others.

Not, Caroline noted in frustration, that this made a difference where the family spoilsport was concerned.

Jack exhaled. "Seriously, Mom, when Cinco de Mayo falls on a Saturday, it makes for a wild and wacky weekend."

That was true. The entertainment industry went all out to celebrate the festivities. Special deals and parties abounded. The occasion was so joyous that no one wanted to be left out.

Patrice gave her son a maternal look that would have quelled even the most unruly son. "Excuse me. How long have I lived in Texas?"

Sensing fireworks about to erupt, Caroline held up a silencing palm and interjected. "You don't have to hold your wedding in the city." Where—Jack was right—holiday traffic and congestion could be a nightmare to navigate. "You could have it at a private ranch, for instance. Under a tent."

"Sounds lovely!" Patrice brightened. "And I really like using Cinco de Mayo as a theme."

"It would make for a lively reception," Dutch said.

Patrice clapped her hands together. "Then it's settled."

Jack wrapped several stacks of corn tortillas in foil, and put them in the oven to heat. He shook his head but said nothing more, merely went to work chopping up a stack of fresh green poblano peppers and sweet yellow onions.

"We also need to talk florists."

"I'll leave that up to you," Patrice said. "Although I'll be in on the selection of flowers. I'm very particular about scent."

Caroline could imagine.

Maddie sashayed up to the table, Bounder by her side. "I want to talk about cake!" she said.

Caroline couldn't help but grin.

Patrice wrapped her arm about her granddaughter's shoulders. "I'm sure Caroline brought pictures of some."

"I certainly did. These bakers I think are particularly excellent." Caroline brought out the brochures with the color photographs.

"I like that one." Maddie pointed to a cake topped with the traditional bride and groom, then looked up at Jack, serious, intent. "Daddy, when are you going to get married? So I can have a mommy, like all my friends."

THE SILENCE FELL in the room so suddenly, Caroline could have heard a pin drop.

Jack looked...uncomfortable, to say the least. He slid the sliced veggies into a sizzling skillet. "Maddie, we talked about this."

Curious, Caroline wondered what exactly had been said. Nothing, it appeared, to Maddie's satisfaction, judging by the pout now on the little girl's face.

"Savannah's daddy married Alexis, and she got a mommy, and she's going to have a little brother or sister, too! Kayla, Ava and Tommy's daddy got married, and they got a new baby! Mia and Sophie's daddy got married, and they got two brothers, Tucker and Tristan. So when is it going to be *my* turn?" Maddie demanded, upset, propping her little hands on her hips.

He seemed temporarily at a loss. Which was not, Caroline figured, a usual state of affairs for the sexy CEO.

Maddie glared at Jack, waiting.

Patrice lifted an elegant blond brow. "Good question," Jack's mother murmured, unsurprised by the outburst. Which meant, Caroline noted, the question had been asked before. Many times. Just not in front of Caroline.

Jack came around the counter to kneel in front of his daughter. "I told you, honey. I was married once, and it didn't work out very well."

Maddie sighed loudly. Her eyes took on a truculent sheen. "You got a divorce and Mommy left."

Jack nodded, confirming this was so, then explained, "Mommy had been married before. And she realized she still loved Cody and wanted to be married to him. So because I wanted her to be happy, I gave her the divorce she wanted and Mommy went to live with Cody again."

"In Costa Rica, which is very, very far away," Maddie repeated, as if this had been told to her many times before. "And she couldn't take me with her because it was better for me to stay here with you and Gram."

Jack nodded. "Right." He patted his daughter comfortingly on the shoulder.

Maddie's lower lip shot out even farther. She stamped her foot. "But how come I can't go see her just for a visit?"

Why not? Caroline wondered, too.

Jack looked at his mother for help on that one. Patrice interjected with maternal sweetness. "You will, darling, one day. When you're older and can travel that far away. In the meantime, you're here with us, and we all love you very much."

"I know." Maddie sighed glumly, only partially mollified. "I love you, too."

Appearing to think the crisis had been averted, Jack rose and went back to his chef duties.

Maddie climbed onto a stool at the counter. She rested her elbows on the counter and cradled her chin in her palms. "I know you and Mommy can't get married again, Daddy—because Mommy is married to Cody now. But I still want a mommy now."

"The only way I can give you an actual mommy is to get married." Jack lifted a meat platter out of the warming oven and set it on the counter. The familiar, homey scent of mesquite-smoked brisket filled the room.

"Then get married!" Maddie advised, as though it were just that simple. Her opinion stated, she slid off the stool and took Bounder out in the sunlit backyard to play.

"MADDIE MIGHT HAVE a point," Patrice said, a moment later.

Feeling as if she were in the middle of a family drama she should not be witnessing, Caroline started to rise. "Perhaps I should step outside, too," she offered cordially.

"Nonsense!" Patrice patted Caroline's forearm and wordlessly directed her to resume her seat. "You're going to be around a lot the next few weeks. And this isn't going to be a secret."

Still feeling like this was far too intimate a situation for her to be witnessing, Caroline reluctantly sat down.

Jack began to carve the hearty slab of beef into long thin strips. "What isn't going to be a secret?"

Patrice glanced through the bay window to make sure Maddie was out of earshot. "The fact that although Dutch and I will still make our home here with you and Maddie, the two of us will also be doing a fair amount of traveling. It's possible we may even be gone weeks or months at a time."

The plan sounded reasonable to Caroline, given the fact the couple was well-off, in their early sixties and Dutch was newly retired.

"Does Maddie know this?" Jack asked calmly.

Caroline began to see the problem.

For the first time, regret showed on Patrice's elegant face. "I thought we would talk to her together."

Worry clouded Jack's eyes.

He wasn't only protective of his mother, Caroline noted, but all the "women" in his family.

"I'd rather not talk to Maddie at all." Jack piled shredded cheese, vegetables and mounds of tender sliced brisket onto serving platters. He paused to give his mother a long, guilt-inducing glance. "I'd rather you stay here and keep your traveling to a minimum, at least in the beginning."

Caroline could see why Jack was concerned, given how much of a change this would be for his daughter.

"I know, dear." Patrice rounded the counter. She poured big glasses of iced tea for the grown-ups and a glass of milk for her granddaughter. She turned to her son, and told Jack kindly but sternly, "I appreciate the way you let me become part of your household after your divorce, but it's time we moved on from that. It's time I went back to living a full life. Time you did, too."

"Meaning?" Jack said, not bothering to disguise his derision.

"I agree with your daughter, Jack. Maddie needs a mother and you need a wife." Patrice paused, making sure she had his full attention. "You need to start dating again—with a view toward marriage."

"SORRY YOU HAD TO hear all that this evening," Jack told Caroline several hours later, when Dutch had gone into the study to return a few business calls and Patrice had gone upstairs with Maddie to supervise the bath and bedtime routine.

Caroline wasn't. It had given her a clear view into what was going on with Jack's family. "It's not a problem." She packed up both her business bags, slung one over her shoulder and carried the other in her hands. "I understand weddings can be stressful. For everyone."

Jack accompanied her to the foyer, held the door for her, then followed her out to her car.

"I'll do what I can to limit the stress for all of you." Caroline dropped both bags into the trunk of her BMW, then shut the lid.

"The only way to do that," Jack muttered unhappily, "is by talking my mom out of this emotionally overwrought, ill-thought-out mistake."

Caroline had just spent the evening with Dutch and Patrice. And while they didn't seem to be wildly *romantically* in love, there was a deep bond between the two, forged by what exactly Caroline didn't know and didn't care. All she knew for certain was that these two sixty-somethings were determined to be together and build a life together as soon as possible. Caroline applauded that kind of determination. And she was in the business of making dreams come true.

There was only one thing standing in their way.

And that big lug of a Texas powerhouse was standing right beside her.

"You know what the problem with you is?" Caroline said before she could stop herself.

One corner of impossibly sensual lower lip curved upward. "No," Jack responded drily, shoving his hands into the pockets of his jeans. He leaned closer, aligning their faces so they were nose to nose. "But I have the feeling you're about to tell me."

The comedic undertone in his low voice only furthered the flame of her temper. Caroline aimed a finger at the center of his chest, in the place where his heart was supposed to be. "You don't have a romantic bone in your body."

He scoffed, rolled his eyes and prodded teasingly, "And you have deduced that because…?"

"For starters?" Caroline stepped closer. This situation had gotten far too personal. And thanks to the unhappy memories Jack's actions were bringing up, her emotions were out of control. So out of control, she found herself blurting out, "You are the kind of all-thought, no-heart guy who can no more appreciate a night like tonight than he can the validity of someone else's dreams!"

He looked around, unimpressed. "What's so special about tonight?"

"Aside from the fact that your mother was planning her ideal nuptials?"

"Aside from that."

Deciding to help him see the romantic side of life, even if it annoyed the heck out of him, Caroline drawled, "Well, for starters, there's a black-velvet sky overhead, sprinkled with stars and a gorgeous half-moon." That alone was enough to bring to mind couples in clinches and hot, passionate kisses.

Ignoring his bemused expression, Caroline pressed on. "Not to mention a warm, humid breeze…" that felt so good, gently caressing their bodies "…and the scent of flowers and fresh-cut grass in the air…." That all added to the wildly reckless feeling of spring.

Caroline turned away from Jack and continued her romantic survey with a wistfulness borne deep inside her. "This neighborhood that you call home is so beautiful, with all the well-kept residences and the peaceful, almost pastoral street." It was everything she had ever wanted and never had.

She whirled back to face him, almost angry now. She stomped closer, waving her arms for emphasis. "But do you see any of that?" Nearer still. "Do you *realize* how lucky you are to live here and have family who have always been there for you and clearly love you so much? No. You don't. You probably look at them, at an incredibly beautiful night like tonight and—"

Caroline never had a chance to finish.

Before the breath left her lungs, Jack swept her into his arms and delivered the kiss to end all kisses. She was so shocked initially she didn't know what to do. And that millisecond of total stillness on her part was all the advantage he needed. The pressure of his mouth parted her lips. His tongue swept inside, and all coherent thought fled. Longing welled up within her, unlike anything she had ever dreamed she could feel. A shiver of need swept through her, followed by an even more magnificent ripple of pure pleasure. Even while her mind protested, the rest of her—heart, body and soul—surrendered to the sweet surprise of his kiss. And the knowledge that maybe, just maybe, she had really misread this man, in thinking that he had no heart…. Because surely it was impossible to kiss with this much ardor, unless you felt…

She leaned closer, emboldened by the ferocity of her own response, wanting, needing, to know and experience more….

And just that suddenly, he released her.

Looking down at her with a distinctly male satisfaction, he surveyed her lazily from head to toe, and taunted softly, "Still think I haven't got a romantic bone in my body?"

# Chapter Three

Jack had the satisfaction of seeing Caroline's jaw open in surprise, a telling moment before it snapped shut. "Sex and romance are not the same thing," Caroline snapped. "And that kiss was pure sex."

And then some, Jack thought, feeling the hardness at the front of his jeans. He was pretty sure from the bright flush of color in her face that she was still tingling from head to toe, too. He edged closer. He might not be much good at love, but there were a few things in which he excelled. "Sex can be good."

"Not between us," Caroline reminded him sternly. "I am now working for your mother and Dutch Ambrose."

He refused to bow to her polite but aloof regard. "I'm the one paying the bill."

"Which makes it even worse," she complained, even as red-hot sparks arced between them. "Technically, *you're* the client." She angled her thumb at her chest. "And I never mix business and pleasure."

Jack grinned. The way she had kissed him back just now said otherwise. "What do you mix with pleasure?" he countered, already thinking of hot kisses and soft skin.

"Nothing." Caroline folded her arms beneath her breasts. She glared at him. "I'm celibate."

"Could have fooled me with that kiss."

She leaned closer, curious. "I take that to mean you do fool around?"

The challenging glitter in her eyes prompted his defense. "Not indiscriminately," Jack replied, inhaling the soft, womanly scent of her. "Although, for the record, I have dated since my divorce. Mainly because I knew at some point Maddie was going to want and need a mommy, the way she is now."

"So you took one for the team," Caroline said drily.

That had been about it. He hadn't been doing it for himself. Jack shrugged, admitting, "There were plenty of women who were interested in my success and wealth. But no one who could deal with how complicated my life has become in recent years." So that had been that.

Now she was interested. She tilted her head. "Complicated in what way?"

How about every way? Jack thought. "Well, my mom lives with me. And if the marriage goes through, soon Dutch will, too. That alone was a turnoff to many."

Caroline's brow furrowed. "I can't see why if they'd met Patrice and/or Dutch."

That, Jack thought, had been the family-inclusive attitude he'd been looking for, and never found. He went on to the next item on the list. "Another bummer was the fact that I can't seem to make long-range or sometimes even short-range plans. Because when I do, something always seems to come up."

Caroline wasn't upset about that, either. "Life happens. I have that problem, too."

They exchanged smiles.

Jack persisted with his wish list. "Anyone I get involved with has to adore Maddie, and be loved by her in return."

Caroline grinned, enthusiastic. "I can't see that as a problem."

Jack went on to the ultimate deal breaker. "And any potential love interest for me must like dogs and accept that Bounder is as much a part of our family as the rest of us. And Bounder can be a handful at times, let me tell you. It seems like she's always inadvertently getting into trouble of some sort."

Caroline rocked back on her heels and angled her chin at him. "That's typical for golden retrievers her age, isn't it? Most don't mature until they are three years old."

Glad to find Caroline so knowledgeable, Jack nodded. "The vet says that we've got another year to go before Bounder gets her natural inquisitiveness under control. Although she is pretty well behaved most of the time now."

"See?" Caroline lifted her hands, palms up. "Life is looking up."

Jack's natural wariness kicked in. "Is it? Maddie still wants a mommy. Now."

Caroline studied him beneath the fringe of her lashes. "And what do you want?" she asked softly.

Jack shrugged. That was easy. "The kind of close and loving marriage my parents had, and the ability to work as a team, no matter how difficult life gets."

So JACK WAS A ROMANTIC at heart, after all, Caroline thought. He just wouldn't acknowledge it. Which made her wonder… "I guess you didn't have that kind of closeness with your ex-wife."

Jack gestured. "We were a great team, while we were together. The problem was…" Jack hesitated.

For a moment Caroline thought he wasn't going to finish.

"As much as she tried, in the end Vanessa couldn't love me as much as she thought she should."

His voice was calm, matter-of-fact, but Caroline sensed a wealth of pain behind those words. She reached out to touch his hand. "I'm sorry," she said, just as quietly, looking deep into his eyes. "I know what it is to be betrayed by someone close to you. It's incredibly demoralizing." It left you reluctant to try love again.

Jack leaned against her BMW. He searched her face. "What happened to you?"

Deciding it might be cathartic to talk about this with Jack, Caroline took the perch next to him. "I was working for an exclusive hotel as an event planner. I was up for a big promotion and I really wanted it." She closed her eyes briefly, remembering that awful time in her life, then turned to look at Jack. "My fiancé concluded I wouldn't have enough time for us if I got it, so he went behind my back and had drinks with my boss and told him that we were planning to start a family shortly after we married, and were even thinking of pushing up our wedding date. Needless to say," Caroline concluded, bitterness welling up inside her, "that man-to-man talk cost me the increase in pay and responsibility. When I found out why I lost out on the professional advancement, I confronted my fiancé."

Jack's lips compressed. He looked as discontented as she felt. "Was your ex apologetic?"

Caroline blew out a gusty breath, shook her head. She traced the paisley pattern on her cotton skirt. "On the contrary. Roark didn't see it as a betrayal. He felt justified in his actions, said he was only thinking of us, and our happiness." Caroline threw up her hands in disgust. "That was it for me. I broke off our engagement and asked Roark to move out of the apartment. I quit my job and started my own wedding planning business. So in the end—"

she finished with a shrug "—it turned out to be a good thing."

Aware she had just given Jack quite a chunk of her life story while she still knew very little about him, she asked in turn, "What about you?" *What happened to break your heart?*

"I fell in love with a beautiful woman who seemed ideal for me in every way. We married and bought a home and had Maddie, and just when everything should have been perfect, Vanessa told me that although she hadn't actually done anything about it, she had never gotten over Cody, her first husband."

Caroline could barely fathom such disloyalty. The hands in her lap stilled. "You must have been devastated."

Jack's mouth took on a rueful curve. He turned his glance to the stars shimmering overhead. "Among other things," he said quietly.

Caroline resisted the romance of the spring evening. "And you never had a clue Vanessa was on the rebound?"

Jack shook his head, his gaze trained on some distant point. "I thought Cody's lack of drive and ambition had killed their marriage, that she was tired of living hand to mouth, of always wondering if they would have enough money to pay the rent."

"Whereas you..." Caroline guessed.

"Worked all the time, at that point, and was rarely if ever off the job. But—" Jack drew in a deep breath, exhaled "—Vanessa was okay with that. In fact—" Jack gestured inanely "—she did everything she could to support and encourage me in that regard."

Except love him, Caroline thought, her heart breaking for Jack. He deserved so much better. They all did. Unable to help herself, she reached over and covered his hand with her own. "Did you love her?"

Jack turned his palm, so their fingers were intertwined. He admitted circumspectly, "I loved who I thought she was…my dream woman."

Aware her heart was racing, Caroline removed her hand from his, sat back, still struggling to understand. "But she wasn't."

"Neither Cody nor Vanessa could meet each other's needs that first time around. As a result, their marriage failed. Wanting a different result in her second marriage, Vanessa was determined to meet all of my needs, even if she had to do so disingenuously. And it worked. I was deliriously happy. She was the one who was miserable. She had everything she had ever wanted, financially, but her whole life felt like a lie. She thought having a baby might change that, give her life more meaning, but it didn't."

"So Vanessa asked you for a divorce."

"Yes. Shortly after we separated, Vanessa got back together with Cody. This time they were wise enough to be able to make it work. The one thing that stood in their way was the baby she'd had with me. Cody didn't like the reminder she'd been with another man. Nor did she. So, for all our sakes, she gave me full custody of Maddie."

It sounded reasonable. And unbearably cruel, Caroline thought, splaying a hand over her chest. "And Vanessa's never seen Maddie since?"

"No. Although, for the record, I've encouraged Vanessa to come and visit or stay in touch in some fashion because I think some contact would be better for Maddie than complete abandonment, but Vanessa thinks otherwise. She and Cody have gone on to have two children of their own, and Vanessa doesn't want to mix her two families."

"But you still expect Maddie and Vanessa to meet one day."

Jack nodded. "I think curiosity will demand it at some point, which is why I continue to lay it out as an option. Although it won't be until Maddie is old enough to understand and handle it."

"I'm sorry," Caroline said finally, her heart going out to him. "You and Maddie deserve so much better."

"So do you," Jack retorted.

Caroline rose gracefully to her feet, turned to face Jack, who was still leaning on her BMW. "I guess that's just life, though. Everyone has bad things happen to them. It doesn't mean we have to give up on our dreams. So if you're interested in getting back out there on the dating scene…"

He held up a palm. "Uh, no."

"Don't trust you'll get it right this time?"

"Do you?" Jack countered, standing, too.

Caroline wasn't used to being put on the defensive by clients. Usually, all people who were getting married wanted to do was talk about themselves, their families, the celebration itself and their hopes for their future, which was fine by her. It meant she didn't have to concentrate on herself, either. "I don't really think about it much," Caroline confessed. Not since she had concluded she had lost out on what could very well be her one chance to have the love of her life. Why? Because ultimately she and Roark hadn't been compatible. And shared values were a key ingredient to any successful relationship.

"Which means you're not actively looking for romance, either," Jack teased with an audacious grin.

Caroline ignored the sudden jump in her pulse, and the fact it would be all too easy to fall in bed with Jack. "Or sex," Caroline pointed out with an arch look that reminded him of the inappropriateness of their earlier embrace.

"Which is a shame," Jack continued with a lusty look meant to provoke. "Since you're an *awfully* good kisser."

Wishing she had met Jack some other time, some other way, Caroline bantered back with utter practicality. "So are you. It doesn't mean we should take that to mean anything other than what it does."

He stepped closer. "Which is what exactly?"

His nearness sent another thrill soaring through her. "Pure and simple? We have chemistry. But again, that doesn't mean we should indulge in it."

Jack lifted a skeptical brow.

With a sigh, Caroline continued explaining. "I love extra-dark chocolate."

"Good to know," Jack replied, smiling.

"If I ate it as much as I'd like to eat it, I'd weigh a ton."

His gaze drifted over her from head to toe, apparently finding nothing wanting. "So you limit yourself," Jack guessed.

Tingling everywhere his eyes had touched, Caroline affirmed her self-imposed sacrifice. "To one treat a week."

Jack's eyes lit up. "I could live with one kiss a week."

The warmth inside her built. Caroline wrinkled her nose. "I couldn't."

The playful moment turned heated again and Caroline could have sworn Jack was thinking about kissing her again. She was not surprised. She was suddenly fantasizing about the same thing.

"Why not?" he quipped.

Blushing fiercely, she tipped her head up. "Because indulging in one kiss a week with you would lead to wanting more than one kiss."

He wrapped his arms around her shoulders. "Also good to know," Jack interrupted with a mischievous grin.

She placed her hand on his chest "And I'm not interested in starting anything with a person I'm not suited to be with long-term."

Jack studied her. "What makes you think we're not compatible?"

Caroline stepped back. He'd given her no choice. She had to be extremely direct. "I'm in the business of making dreams come true." Their eyes met and held for another breath-stealing moment. "And unless you've changed your mind about Patrice marrying Dutch, you're now in the business of thwarting them."

"I'VE NOTICED," Patrice Gaines said the next morning when Caroline showed up promptly at eight-thirty, still reeling from the ill-advised kiss she had shared with Jack Gaines the previous evening, "that you don't wear perfume."

Telling herself it was definitely going to be possible to stay away from the ruggedly handsome businessman while planning his mother's wedding, Caroline smiled self-consciously. She forced herself to concentrate on the conversation at hand. "That must seem like heresy to a woman like you, who built her fortune on perfume."

Patrice gently acknowledged this was so. "May I ask why you don't wear any?"

A little embarrassed by the oversight, given the company she was keeping, Caroline shrugged. "I guess I've never found a fragrance that really suits me. They always seem too heavy, or too young, or too musky…too something."

Patrice smiled. "Whereas I don't feel fully dressed unless I have a fragrance on."

Caroline opened up her briefcase. "I've noticed you wear different scents."

Patrice brought a thermal carafe of coffee to the breakfast table. "For different moods."

Caroline set up her laptop computer. "It must be nice to be able to create your own colognes."

Patrice went back to the cupboard to get mugs. "I could do it for you, as a thank-you, for working us in on such short notice."

Caroline laid the sample invitations and the accompanying price list on the table. "I didn't know you still created individual perfume formulas."

Patrice returned with cream and sugar. "I can't for financial gain. It's in the contract I signed with Couture Perfume. But I can do it for fun," she continued enthusiastically, "and I'd really like to try."

Caroline dipped her head in silent thanks. "I'd be honored."

Patrice settled opposite her. "So when do you want to start?"

Caroline accepted the mug of hot coffee. "Start?"

Patrice stirred a spoonful of sugar into her coffee. "We're going to have to sit down and go through the various fragrance families. Although I must warn you—once we find the exact right scent, and you begin wearing it, you will have men falling in love with you constantly."

"It's true." Dutch walked in to join them. He wrapped his arm around Patrice's shoulders. "I've seen it happen."

Caroline studied the handsome older couple. "Is that how the two of you fell in love?"

Patrice and Dutch tensed almost imperceptibly. They turned to each other, looked into each other's eyes in silent understanding. Confirming, Caroline thought, Jack's suspicion that something other than the expected was behind this union. But that didn't mean it was wrong. Companionship and compatibility were wonderful reasons to get married, too, especially when the bride and groom were old enough to have experienced life and know what really counted. "It's complicated," Patrice said finally.

"And astoundingly wonderful and generous and right." Dutch pulled Patrice toward him for a quick kiss on her brow.

The two fell silent, still gazing tenderly and meaningfully at one another.

There was love there, Caroline surmised, just not the head-over-heels kind younger brides and grooms typically exhibited.

From the doorway, a throat cleared. Jack stood there in a blue oxford cloth shirt and khaki slacks. It was clear from the expression on his face that he had heard everything. And was no more reassured that this was indeed an advisable union than he had been before.

Jack looked at his mother. "Maddie said you needed to see me before I took her to school this morning."

Patrice informed him casually, "I'm not going to be able to go with Caroline to view those two ranches, where our wedding could be held, so I'm going to need you to do it for me."

Jack looked simultaneously stunned and put out. Caroline couldn't say she blamed him. This was short notice.

Jack frowned. "Can't you go another time?"

"Caroline says we need to have the time and place locked in before we do anything else, and since I assumed you'd want to have a say as well as read the contract…"

Dutch glanced at his watch, then leaned in and lightly touched Patrice's arm. "I've got to make a call," he murmured. Patrice nodded agreeably while Dutch slipped out.

Jack continued to look at his mother with very little patience. "I've got a business to run," he reminded her.

"And I completely forgot I promised Maddie's teacher I would help out at her school this morning."

"Can't Dutch go?"

Patrice held her ground. "You're the one who has to okay the financial terms, dear."

Jack slowly let out his breath, his love for his mother as evident as his exasperation. Lips thinning, he said, "I'll just call the office and let them know I won't be in."

JACK WAS HALFWAY through the study doors when he heard Dutch's voice and realized Dutch was just outside the window, talking on his cell phone.

"May I speak to Maryellen? I understand. Just tell her it's Dutch. I'll meet her at the apartment, usual time. And please remind her of the need for privacy. I don't want anyone to know.... Thank you." Dutch ended the call.

Maryellen? Jack thought, stunned. What apartment? Why did Dutch and Maryellen need privacy? What was so secret? Was Dutch having an affair with this woman? And if so, what was he supposed to do about it? It wasn't as if he could—or would even want—to say anything to his mother without first knowing exactly what the situation was.

Feeling more conflicted than ever, Jack shut the doors, then dialed the private investigator who did the background checks for his company. He explained to Laura Tillman what was going on.

"It's too late for me to get someone out there right now," she said.

"Maybe I should tail him," Jack offered.

"Don't," Laura directed sternly. "You're not a professional. If Dutch is hiding something, you'll only alert him to the fact you overheard something you clearly should not have. You've got almost three weeks before the wedding actually happens. Let us do this."

Jack sighed. He knew she was right. But it left him feeling powerless. He did not like it. He wanted to be able to protect his loved ones, no matter what the circumstances.

There was a rap behind him. The study door opened. His mother pointed to her watch, then waved, along with Maddie. Smiling, the two left.

"Jack? Are you still there?" the P.I. said.

Out in the driveway, Dutch's car started, then Jack's mother's. "I'm here," Jack said, as Caroline appeared near the doorway, too, a question in her eyes. "You've got my approval," Jack said firmly. "Just do what has to be done as quickly as possible." In his view, there wasn't a moment to lose.

"SORRY ABOUT THAT," Caroline said as Jack joined her. "Your mother suggested I hurry you along or you'd be on the phone with your office forever."

Which reminded Jack…he hadn't called in to his secretary yet. "I've still got one more call to make," he said.

Jack would have been annoyed in her place, but Caroline looked at Jack with the patience of a saint. "I'll wait in the living room," she said.

Jack wrapped up business as quickly as he could. It still took fifteen minutes.

Caroline was on her laptop busily typing away when he joined her again. She held up a hand, finished what she was doing, then shut down her computer.

"So where are we going?" Jack asked as they walked out to her car. She slid behind the wheel, turned on the car and activated the sedan's directional system, keying in their destination in the GPS.

Her silk blouse pulling across the soft curves of her breasts, Caroline checked to make sure the way was clear, then backed out of the drive.

Unable to help but note the way her skirt rode up her thighs as her foot moved from accelerator to brake, Jack turned his attention to the street ahead.

Oblivious to how aware he was of her, Caroline continued talking business. "Thus far, I've only located two venues that can handle an outdoor wedding and reception on short notice. The first—Wedding Bells Ranch—is an hour north of the city, and just opened a couple of months ago."

Even the name sounded cheesy, Jack thought with disdain. He turned to shoot her a curious look. A copper-colored strand of hair had fallen across her cheek, partially obscuring the dainty freckles that speckled her high, elegant cheekbones. He ignored the urge to capture the silky strand and tuck it behind her ear. "Have you ever been there?" he asked, forcing himself to concentrate on his task, rather than his attractive companion.

"No." Caroline accelerated smoothly and merged onto the freeway. "The photos on their Web site look great, although those can be deceiving."

Jack appreciated the deft way she negotiated the heavy city traffic. "Did you check with the Better Business Bureau?"

"Yes. So far, they've had no negative reporting but, as I said, the site has only been open a few months."

"And the other location?"

Her brows knit together. "Is a little over an hour and twenty minutes due west of the city."

Jack calculated the mileage and the time it would take to see both. He frowned.

Caroline held up a silencing hand. "I realize this is

probably going to take a big chunk out of both our days, unless the first place works out to your satisfaction."

Knowing time was money, Jack said, "Then we'll hope for the first."

Caroline took the exit that would lead them to the countryside. Still all business, she slanted him a glance. "Aren't you interested in price differential?"

Traffic instantly became much less intense. Jack relaxed in the bucket seat. "Is there one?"

She nodded. "The second place is ten percent less. But… the bride and groom need to think about the convenience of their guests. Sometimes if a venue is too far away, guests opt out of attending, especially in Dutch and Patrice's age group."

"True." Traveling, Jack knew, was harder on his mother these days than it had been in the past. Which made her determination to be on the road so much more puzzling, to say the least. Especially since his mother and Dutch weren't traveling much at all now. "Then let's hope the first place works out," he said.

IT WAS SO MUCH WORSE than what Caroline had imagined, even in a worst-case scenario. And nothing like the gloriously beautiful pictures on the Wedding Bells Ranch Web site.

"Can we sue them for false advertising?" Jack joked as they got out of the car.

Caroline wished she could feel similarly amused. Since she had just been professionally humiliated in front of a man she really wanted to impress, for reasons that had little to do with the business at hand, it wasn't possible.

"We should just forget it," Jack said in disgust.

Caroline's conscience wouldn't let her do that. She had

made an appointment. She would follow through, if only briefly. "If you'd rather wait in the car…"

Jack looked at the peeling paint on the ranch house and barn, the broken-down steps and weed-ridden lawn. "If you're going up there—" he pointed to the elaborate sign that said Wedding Bells Ranch Office "—so am I."

Together, Caroline and Jack walked through the crabgrass to the door.

Knocked. The door opened. A pretty young woman in paint-splattered jeans and a T-shirt opened the door. "Caroline Mayer, I presume." She started to extend a hand, then stopped, realizing her fingers were splattered with wet paint. "Hi. I'm Lysette Beasley. Owner. As you can see, we are a work in progress, but I promise you we will be up and running by the end of the summer."

"My client is getting married in three weeks," Caroline said.

"Three!" Lysette clapped a hand to her chest in surprise. "I saw May 5 on your e-mail appointment request. I guess the year didn't compute. I just assumed… Who plans a wedding in *three* weeks?"

"My mother and her fiancé," Jack said, grim as ever on the subject.

"Oh. Dear." Lysette looked all the more distressed.

"Oh, dear" was right, Caroline thought.

"Even under a tent, I don't think there is any way we could be ready to hold a big gala by then," Lysette Beasley said.

Caroline sighed, and took another look around. "I would have to agree."

"What about the photos on the Web site?" Jack asked.

"Those were computer mock-ups of how we want the place to look, when I'm finished renovating," Lysette said.

"You should put a disclaimer on the site," Caroline said, making no effort to disguise her disappointment.

Lysette wrinkled her nose. "People keep telling me that. But I don't know. I think it might cost me business."

Jack snorted.

"Having people feel you've duped them will cost you business," Caroline muttered.

Caroline and Jack headed back to her BMW.

"Honest misunderstanding," Jack soothed Caroline with unexpected understanding. He reached over to briefly take her hand. "Anyone could make it."

Caroline looked at Jack. Fingers still tingling from the brief unexpected touch, she said, "We'll try the next one and hope we have a lot better luck."

# Chapter Four

"It's a sign," Jack said nearly two hours later when they finally had arrived at their destination and completed a tour, which had taken all of five minutes.

Caroline had an idea how Jack was seeing this locale. It was out in the middle of nowhere, surrounded by other ranches and the occasional small enclave with a few houses, a gas station, post office, church and a general store. To her, though, this flat, barren land that stretched as far as the eye could see—with the picturesque outcroppings of blooming wildflowers, cactus, sage and mesquite—was quintessential Texas, perfect for a Mexican-festival-themed wedding at sunset. She gazed thoughtfully at their surroundings, already picturing where everything would go. Chairs here, wedding gazebo here, dinner tents here, stage for the band and dance floor there—additional flats of Texas wildflowers there. There was so much space they could have one heck of a party.

Aware Jack was watching her as carefully as she was surveying the land, awaiting her reply, she turned back to him with a small shrug and an officious smile. "I don't believe in signs."

The corners of his mouth turned down into a scowl. "How about fate, then?" He continued looking around with displeasure.

Caroline brought out her notepad and pen and scrawled a few reminders to herself. Her mind was already made up. "Do you really think I'd be reaching so far outside the realm if it weren't for the purpose of making your mother and Dutch's dream come true?"

Jack scoffed and ran a hand through his hair. "This is outside the realm, all right."

Caroline walked slightly ahead to admire the view toward the west, in the direction the sun would set. She paced out to where she thought the actual ceremony should take place, next to a meadow filled with bluebonnets. "The land is flat." Trying not to notice how his tall, broad-shouldered frame dwarfed her, Caroline continued to make her case for this venue. "All the better to create a parking area, erect the tents and set up a big dance floor."

Jack stood, legs braced apart, arms folded in front of him. His eyes darkened with pure disdain. "We're twenty miles from the nearest town. And there are no bathrooms."

Caroline made another note to check pricing on that. "So we'll haul in Porta Potties."

Jack's jaw dropped open in shock. "At my mother's wedding?" He looked at her as if she were nuts.

Caroline wrinkled her nose at him. "Not the yellow kind you see at construction sites and outdoor concerts, silly. The ultraelegant air-conditioned kind housed in trailers that can be hooked up to the campground-style water and power supply the ranch provides. We can set them up around the perimeter, and they'll form a nice buffer against the highway, so that the view from there will be obscured, giving the wedding party total privacy."

That idea, Jack appeared to like. Which didn't surprise her. He seemed like a quiet, private type of guy. Still waters ran deep, and all that. To the point she was willing to bet that despite his foray into dating, he hadn't been really close to anyone—in a romantic sense—since his wife had taken off with her ex-husband. The difference between Jack and Caroline was that Caroline had actually tried getting close to someone again. It was just none of the men she had met had really interested her, and things had always fizzled out after the first or second date, never really going anywhere by mutual consent.

She had been starting to think that she just didn't have it in her anymore for a sexy romantic relationship, and hence, had decided to stop worrying about it. She would simply never have a man in her life again.

She would still be in that particular mindset, had Jack not kissed her the other night, and shown her that her desire was still in fine working order.

Too bad she and Jack were on such different pages otherwise.

Had she not been planning his mother's wedding—and had he still not been hoping the event would somehow be derailed—something fun and exciting might have been possible between them.

But that wasn't likely to happen, so she had to turn her thoughts back to the event, and concentrate on his endless supply of questions.

"What about food?" Jack asked, still frowning.

Caroline looked at him in profile. From the side he was just as fetching, in that scientifically smart "engineer cute" way. Telling her libido to cool down—obviously the hours spent in close quarters in her car had stirred up her hormones again—Caroline replied in her usual precise, businesslike tone that she knew the CEO in Jack would appreciate. "We can haul in portable gas stoves and Sub-Zero refrigerators. Chef For Hire in Fort Worth does just that."

Jack smiled for the first time since getting out of her car. "I know. My buddy Dan's wife, Emily, owns that business."

Another connection between the two of them, heretofore, gone unnoticed. How strange was that? "If Emily can do it, we would be all set."

Not so fast, Jack's expression seemed to say. He paced the dusty gravel road that served as the driveway into the party ranch. "Did you notice there are big cattle ranches on nearly all sides of the place?"

Yes, Caroline had.

"If the wind hits just right, the whole reception could smell like cow manure."

Caroline couldn't help it; she laughed. "You really are a pessimist," she chided.

Jack narrowed his eyes and strode close enough that she got a whiff of soap and man. "I prefer to think of myself as a realist."

Even so. Caroline reached out and patted his arm. "I think we're going to be fine."

The ranch owner, a burly fellow named Ted with a handlebar mustache and scraggly goatee, was leaning against his pickup some distance away, a toothpick in his mouth. Having no interest or affinity for agriculture, he'd given up ranching the property he had inherited, torn down all the barbed wire fence as well as the ramshackle house that had been on the property, and turned the one-hundred-and-fifty-acre spread into one large grassy area. Complete with meadows of picturesque wildflowers, it was suitable for parties and gatherings of all kinds. The key selling points to his setting were few restrictions and low price—both of which, in Caroline's mind, more than made up for the lack of amenities, which could be rented and brought in.

"Think of this as a blank slate, upon which we can build

your mother's fantasy nuptials," she advised. It was going to be so much easier to create a Cinco de Mayo theme here than in the traditional wedding venues, which were already booked anyway.

Jack sighed. "See what kind of cancellation policy you can work out. I want to be able to get most of our money back if the ceremony doesn't happen."

It was Caroline's turn to scowl at him. "Don't talk that way. You could jinx the wedding."

Jack looked as if he hoped he would.

Irritated by his lack of faith in his mother, Caroline paused to send Jack a withering glance, then stalked off.

She negotiated with the owner of Ted's Party Ranch for a good ten minutes. Finally, she returned to Jack's side. She handed him the contract with the scribbled numbers. "This is the best I could do, and considering it's on a Saturday night on Cinco de Mayo, it's a bargain."

Jack studied the pages with a businessman's assessing eye.

"He wants a five-hundred-dollar deposit to hold it for you. The rest is payable the day of the event, or as soon as we start bringing in the trailers. Given the logistics, I think we're probably going to want to start setting up the tents and so on the day before. And that's okay with Ted. The place is free then, too."

Jack got out his checkbook. "If it rains, we're all going to be miserable," he predicted.

"If you don't stop with the doom and gloom, we won't have to wait for rain to be miserable. We'll all be that way now."

He looked at her with a mixture of resentment and amusement. "Is that the way you talk to a client?"

Caroline patted him on the arm, one potential friend to another. "It's the way I talk to you." She gave that a moment to sink in. "Cheer up, Jack. Your mother is a smart woman. I have every confidence she knows exactly what she is doing in marrying Dutch. And if you give yourself half a chance to look past your own failed marriage, soon you'll know it, too."

As soon as they reached Jack's home in Fort Worth, he headed onto One Trinity River Place to continue supervising the work there. Caroline went inside to talk with Patrice, and show her what they had accomplished thus far.

Patrice had no problem imagining the festivities. She was pleased that a location had been found, a deposit put down. "The only drawback I can see," Patrice said, "is the distance from the city."

"I've thought about that," Caroline said. "I didn't know how you would feel, but I was thinking we could arrange for cars and drivers to transport those who need the assistance from the city and back again."

"That sounds wonderful."

"And there's something else. I had a call from *Fort Worth* magazine. They heard you're getting married and doing a Cinco de Mayo theme, and they want to include your nuptials in an article about unusual Texas weddings. You wouldn't have to do anything except sign a release allowing photographs and details of the ceremony to be published. The magazine would send a reporter and a photographer out to the wedding site to cover the ceremony and reception."

Patrice smiled. "I think it's a wonderful idea. And great publicity for you, dear, as I will insist they mention you as the genius behind the festivities."

Caroline flushed with happiness. "You don't have to do that," she protested.

"Nonsense." Patrice patted Caroline's hand. "It would

be my pleasure. We're both businesswomen. We know the value of good publicity. One positive mention in the press can bring in tons of new business."

That was true, Caroline thought.

It was nice having Jack's mom cheering her on.

Maddie skipped up, her dog, Bounder, right beside her. The seven-year-old had a wreath of silk flowers on her head. Her golden retriever wore one around her neck, too. Maddie picked up a handful of blossoms from the basket over her arm. "Me and Bounder are practicing being flower girls!"

Caroline looked at Jack's mom.

Patrice chuckled and explained, "I've agreed to let them do it together."

Caroline was not surprised. Beloved family pets were often part of the ceremony.

"Do you think that Daddy will let us do it when he gets married, too?" Maddie asked her grandmother.

"I imagine, if and when that ever happens, your daddy would be only too ready to agree," Patrice replied.

Or in other words, Caroline amended silently to herself while simultaneously congratulating Patrice on her tact, don't hold your breath waiting for Jack to ever want to trust again.

And without trust, there could be no love.

Without love, no real, lasting relationship, no true compatibility or companionship, never mind marriage!

"What about you?" Maddie asked, sprinkling another handful of flowers over the wide plank pine floor. Maddie paused directly in front of Caroline. "When you get married, can Bounder and I be your flower girls?"

"Maddie!" Patrice interjected.

"It's okay." Caroline lifted a palm before Patrice could correct her granddaughter. "I can't think of any two 'ladies'

I'd rather have as my flower girls," Caroline said warmly. Then she added for good measure, "If and when I ever marry. Right now I don't even have a boyfriend."

"My daddy doesn't have a girlfriend. So maybe you could be his girlfriend and he could be your boyfriend and that way you'd both have one!"

Caroline chuckled, appreciating the precocious little girl's logic. "What did you say you want to be when you grow up?" She winked. "A matchmaker, per chance?"

"A bride and a princess and a cowgirl!" Maddie shouted, then skipped off, spewing flowers, doggie in tow.

"Sorry about that," Patrice apologized.

"I think she's adorable," Caroline said, watching the little girl race out into the backyard to play in the gorgeous spring weather. "Jack and you and Dutch are lucky to have her in your lives. And her dog is precious, too." Caroline didn't think she had ever seen a pet so utterly devoted to her little mistress.

Patrice followed the direction of Caroline's glance, then focused on her expression. "You really want children, don't you?"

Unable to suppress her wistfulness, Caroline nodded. "My dream is to one day have a little girl of my own, whether I marry or not. I miss having a mom, having a family, having that special mother-daughter bond…and even if I never marry, I know I can still have that."

Patrice nodded, understanding the tick of the biological clock and the fierce yearning to be a mother. "It's even better," Patrice said, "when that mother-daughter bond is three-generational."

"I can imagine." Caroline relaxed. "Although I was never lucky enough to have it. My own grandmother was gone by the time I was old enough to have remembered her."

Patrice reached over and patted Caroline's hand with maternal kindness. "That's a shame. I am sure she would have delighted in you," Patrice said.

The older woman's approval not only meant a lot to Caroline, it radiated in the region of her heart. Maybe because Caroline sensed that Patrice wasn't one to hand out compliments like that idly.

The back door opened and Maddie dashed back in. She plopped down on the carpet and began gathering up the silk petals she had left lying in her wake. While she put them back in her wicker flower girl basket, she asked Caroline, "Do you like weddings?"

"I certainly do. That's why I plan them."

Maddie paused to pet her dog's golden mane. "My daddy doesn't like them."

Patrice countered gently but firmly, "Your daddy is going to like this one, when he gets used to the idea."

So, Caroline thought, Jack's mother knows the extent of her son's disapproval…and was carrying on with her own wishes anyway. Good for her.

Patrice reached over and gently touched Caroline's arm. She winked, woman to woman, and said so only Caroline could hear, "Don't worry. He'll come around."

Caroline hoped so. Otherwise, it wouldn't be the happy day it should be for the Gaines family.

Before anything else could be said, Jack and Dutch walked in. Jack seemed to know immediately he'd been the topic of conversation. Jack looked from Caroline to Patrice and back again. "What's going on?" he asked casually.

"I want you and Caroline to get married!" Maddie declared.

For a moment, everyone was shocked to the point of speechlessness. "I think what she means is she thinks we each should be married," Caroline said, deliberately misinterpreting the little girl's remarks. Her face heating self-consciously, Caroline told Maddie gently, "And before I can be a bride, I have to find someone I could be compatible with, someone who would provide the kind of companionship I'm looking for."

"Maybe my daddy can help you find all that!"

Jack choked in mid-breath. "Maddie!"

Maddie turned back to her daddy. "That way everyone would be happy."

Jack's face was set in stone. "I don't have to be married to be happy, Maddie."

"But I don't have a mommy, and if Gram leaves to go on her honeymoon and her trips with Dutch...who's going to brush my hair and help me put my barrettes in?"

Caroline could see the talk Jack and Patrice had obviously given Maddie on the subject had not gone well. "We'll hire a nanny to help us out temporarily, whenever Gram is gone," Jack said.

Maddie's lower lip slid out. "I don't want a nanny."

Jack promptly reassured, "Then we'll ask a friend."

Maddie's face lit up. "Like Caroline?" she asked eagerly.

Talk about one-track minds, Caroline thought, all the more embarrassed as the adults in the room stifled bemused laughter.

"We'll find someone you like," Jack promised.

Maddie crossed her arms in front of her and glared. "I think I'd rather have Caroline."

"SORRY ABOUT THAT," Jack said after his mother and Dutch had taken Maddie into the backyard.

Caroline looked at Jack sympathetically. There were times, she knew, when being a single parent could be tough.

"I gather Maddie didn't take the news of her grandmother's impending travels well?"

Jack went to the fridge and got out two bottles of chilled spring water. "Mom and I talked to her last night. Maddie said she understood what we were telling her but she really didn't like it." He exhaled. "I guess she's worried—about all those things important to little girls, like getting her hair brushed and the placement of her barrettes."

Their hands brushed briefly as he handed her the drink. Aware that every time she got near Jack her heartbeat sped up and her senses got sharper, Caroline shrugged and said, "Both are simple things to learn, even for a guy."

"You don't think I need a woman to do that for me?"

Deciding she had looked into Jack's eyes far too long, Caroline turned her glance away. "Obviously, you'll need a regular sitter to watch Maddie after school or during those times when you have to work and she's not otherwise occupied, when your mom is off exploring the world with Dutch."

Promising herself she was not going to fall prey to the attraction simmering between them, she looked into the rugged contours of his handsome face. Calling on her own experience as the child of a single mom, she advised, "But I think it's better for Maddie if the two of you figure out how to be a team and cope on your own." They'd be all the stronger for it. "Besides, it's possible your mother and Dutch won't stay away all that long."

Jack's mouth flattened into a grim line. "She seems determined."

To make a point with you, Caroline thought. That you need a fuller, happier life, too.

The patio door opened and closed. Dutch and Patrice walked into the kitchen. "Maddie okay?" Jack asked.

They nodded. "Her friend from next door came over to play," Patrice said.

Jack looked at his mother. "I wish you would delay any extensive traveling until Maddie has more time to get used to the idea."

Dutch gave Patrice a look that seemed to tell his fiancée to proceed with caution.

Caroline lauded the older gentleman's sensitivity to the situation.

Patrice frowned, then turned back to Jack and continued gently but firmly. "Darling, I know you don't want to think about it, but none of us are getting any younger, and Dutch and I want to enjoy whatever time we have left to the absolute fullest."

Jack was right, Caroline noted. His mother was determined not just to marry, but to expand her horizons again in a positive, healthy way.

"I'm not trying to deny you a full life," Jack countered. His brows furrowed in consternation. "But why does it have to be such a big change, so quickly? Why can't you just take a honeymoon and then plan a couple of short trips, maybe to South Padre Island where Dutch owns all those properties?"

Jack had a point, too, Caroline thought. There was something to be said for not taking on too much change at once. Just getting married was a pretty big step. To change one's entire lifestyle, too, and be separated from one's family, could bring on a lot of stress.

Patrice waived off the suggestion with an airy hand. "Dutch is in the process of selling those."

"Why would you want to do that?" Jack asked in surprise.

With a beleaguered frown, Dutch admitted, "South Padre Island is not the quiet oasis it was when I first began to invest there years ago. These days, the area is overrun with college students looking to party."

"Is that the only reason?" Jack asked.

Clearly irked by the nosy query, Patrice gave Jack a reprimanding glance.

Dutch, however, seemed to welcome the chance to be more straightforward with his future stepson. "There were other considerations as well, prompting me to make this move."

"The hurricane that hit that particular area of the Gulf two years ago," Jack guessed.

Dutch nodded. "The losses were catastrophic, even with insurance."

Patrice frowned. "Don't get me started on insurance companies. I thought it was difficult getting them to pay out when your father was ill, Jack, but it's nothing compared to now." She shook her head, incensed. "These days, the jackals will deny you coverage at the drop of a hat. They only want to insure the people who demonstrate no risk of causing them to pay out on anything." Patrice threw up her hands and continued to vent her frustration emotionally. "It doesn't matter if you want to live at the beach, or you're sick, or you have one too many fender benders. The companies will deny you coverage. Or if they do deign to cover you, they will charge you such an outrageous amount it's ridiculous!"

Caroline knew that was true. Rates for older people increased phenomenally, for health, auto and life, at a time when most saw their incomes diminishing. She knew the business reasons why companies did this. Morally, though, it seemed wrong to take advantage of the older population that way. No wonder Patrice was upset.

Dutch reached over and took Patrice's hand in his, simultaneously soothing and silencing his fiancée. Once again, something passed between the two seniors. Perhaps a life experience, Caroline thought, that they did not wish to share. Maybe just the hardship of getting older.

"In any case," Dutch went on, "I prefer to sell and get out of the home rental business now so it's not something I have to worry about later."

Jack nodded. "As a businessman, I can understand that. Just as I'm sure you can understand why I want to see you and my mother sign a prenuptial agreement."

"We agree," Patrice said to Jack's obvious relief.

"We don't want any mingling of our individual assets," Dutch said.

Patrice nodded. "So we've already hired lawyers, one for each of us."

"Naturally, if it'll make you feel better, I'd like you to review all documents prior to signing," Dutch offered sincerely.

"I will," Jack said. "Thank you."

Once again, Caroline felt as if she were witnessing a family drama she'd rather not.

Patrice looked at Caroline. "I meant to tell you. The bakery called to schedule the cake tasting and I set it up for this evening."

"Wonderful!" Caroline smiled, happy to be back on track once again. "We can't get these details wrapped up too soon."

"It's at six-thirty and we'd like you to go," Patrice continued.

Caroline smiled. "That's my job."

"And Jack, too," Patrice added, as if it were the most natural thing in the world.

Not to Jack, however. "Whoa!"

Patrice exercised her maternal imperative. "Darling, you have to. Dutch and I can't handle all that rich food at once. Without a proper tasting of all the choices, how else will we know that we've selected the right confections for our special day?"

Caroline pushed aside the sensual image of tasting cake with Jack. This job was beginning to feel far too familiar for comfort. It was up to her to make sure that the boundaries were still in place. "If it would be more comfortable for you, we can go to the bakery at different times and compare notes later," she told Jack.

"Sounds like a lot of extra work for all concerned to me," Patrice commented.

To Jack, too. He exhaled, the reluctant warrior doing what he had to do, once again. "Of course I'll go with Caroline," he said.

He just did not look happy about it.

## Chapter Five

"You can stop scowling now," Caroline said as she and Jack got out of their cars and met on the sidewalk in front of the row of stores on Sundance Square.

The frown lines on either side of Jack's lips deepened. He looked like most grooms overwhelmed by wedding details. Only problem was, he wasn't the groom. Just the person getting stuck with all the decisions, by default.

Jack shoved his hands in his pockets and strolled down the street of the historic shopping district in downtown Fort Worth. "She's just doing this to get my goat," he muttered.

Caroline had the impression there might be a little payback, too. She fell into step beside him and they headed toward the bakery. "Well, it seems to be working," she drawled, slanting her head at Jack. Jack was taking part in the planning of his mother's wedding, whether he wanted to or not. And that had to make Patrice happy.

Jack's lips tightened in frustration. "She's just annoyed because I brought up the need for a prenuptial agreement."

"You ought to feel happy about that since they've already agreed to get one and let you see it."

Jack looked even more disgruntled. "Not necessarily."

Caroline furrowed her brow in irritation. Would Jack never give it a rest? "What do you mean?" she asked.

Jack stopped and leaned against the plate glass window in front of a golf equipment store with Spring Sale banners plastered across the front. He folded his arms across the hard muscles of his chest. "I had a prenup with Vanessa, too. It was her idea." He paused and looked deep into Caroline's eyes. "It didn't guarantee us a happy marriage."

"Nothing can do that," Caroline returned gently. When people got married, they had to hold on to their dreams and jump in with both feet and hope everything turned out all right. Making a lifetime commitment to someone carried with it an enormous risk. A lot of couples took the danger in stride. Others got nervous about failing and called the whole thing off at the last minute. Caroline did not think Dutch and Patrice were part of the latter group. Which meant nothing Jack could do or say would change their minds. Obviously, his inability to protect his mother from potential harm was very frustrating for him. Caroline couldn't fault Jack for that. She didn't want to see anyone she cared about hurt, either.

"So you think Dutch is out to swindle your mother out of her fortune?"

"He's selling all his beachfront property. Property," Jack emphasized, "that he's held on to for thirty-some years, regardless of how many hurricanes and tropical storms rolled through the area."

Caroline admitted that might be worrisome had Dutch not been in the process of retiring from his life's work. "Dutch intimated it's become too much to manage at this point in his life."

Jack remained suspicious. "You can hire people to do that for you. Dutch knows that." Jack paused and gave Caroline a steady assessing look that had her pulse jumping.

"No, there's more to it than what Dutch and my mom are saying. I'm not sure how much she knows of what is going on, but one way or another, I am going to find out why Dutch is so intent on rushing my mother into marriage." Jack resumed walking.

Caroline raced to catch up and fell in beside him. "They've told you. They're not getting any younger and they want to enjoy whatever time they have left—however many years that turns out to be—together."

"There's more to the story than that." Undeterred, Jack stopped in front of the bakery and held the door for her.

Acutely aware of him, Caroline swept inside.

Jericho, the master baker, was waiting for them. He was dressed in his usual white chef's coat, jeans and boots. A red bandana tied around his head covered all but the ends of his dreadlocks.

"Hey, sweetie," Jericho called out to Caroline in his lilting Jamaican-accented voice. "Good to see you."

Caroline went forward and gave the six-foot man a big hug. The two of them had started their businesses about the same time. Both operations were taking off. Smiling, Caroline introduced Jack to Jericho.

"So—" Jericho gestured for the two of them to take a seat at the retro silver-edged counter "—I hear the wedding has a Cinco de Mayo theme."

Jack looked pained by yet another of his mother's decisions. "I know it's unusual."

Jericho had the opposite view. "Sounds fun," he said. "As well as challenging."

Caroline told the baker the preliminary guest list was now topping out at three hundred, the majority of whom were expected to attend. "What would you suggest we do?"

Jericho brought out a portfolio of his designs and a tray

of cake bites to sample. "Depends on how fun you want to go."

"Knowing my mother? As fun as possible," Jack said.

"That's the spirit!" Jericho said, choosing to mistake Jack's grudging participation for enthusiasm. He offered both of them two square-shaped bites of cake. "So...I was thinking...how about a chapel-shaped *dulce de leche* wedding cake and a sombrero- and serape-shaped devil's food cake for the groom?"

"I'm not sure about the flavors, but I think they'll love the designs," Caroline said.

Jack studied the rough sketches Jericho had produced. "They'd be great for a party, but I'm not certain either is appropriate for a wedding."

Jack was a linear guy. Caroline supposed she should have expected him to take that view. Still, this wasn't his wedding, and Dutch and Patrice wanted everything to be fun.

Caroline opened her mouth to argue the subject with Jack. His cell phone chimed. He looked at the caller ID screen and frowned. "Excuse me. I have to take this." He walked a little distance away. "Hey, Mom. What's up?"

He listened. "Okay, first thing. *Get Maddie away from the scene.* I know, Mom, but she doesn't need to see this. And then do what you can to stop the bleeding. I'll be right there."

He ended the connection. "Got to go. Bounder's hurt."

Unable to bear the thought of the adorable dog in pain, Caroline dashed after Jack. "What happened?"

"Mom and Dutch aren't sure. They put Bounder out back while Maddie was having her bath. When they went to let her in, she was lying on the patio, and there were bloody paw prints all around her. Obviously, Bounder's hurt at least one foot, but they can't tell which one, and she's so upset, she won't let anyone touch her. Dutch and Mom have been trying to get a closer look but they can't catch Bounder—she keeps running away from them. And Maddie's hysterical. I could hear her sobbing in the background."

Her heart going out to all of them, Caroline struggled to keep pace as Jack rushed toward his car. "Sounds like you need help."

Jack shot her a grateful look. "You offering?"

Caroline nodded.

"Then let's go. We'll take my car and come back and get yours later."

Jack climbed behind the wheel of his SUV. He got them "home" in record time. Bypassing the front door, he headed through the gate to the backyard. Adrenaline pumping, Caroline was right behind him.

Bounder was curled up behind Maddie's swing set. When she saw Jack, the golden retriever whimpered, stood. But when he started to approach, she took off again.

Dutch was on the patio, kneeling, a box of dog treats in his hand. "I've been trying to tempt her," Dutch said, concerned. "She's not interested."

"She's scared." Caroline kicked off her heels and walked barefoot through the grass, talking softly all the while. "Oh, my poor Bounder. What happened to you, girl? How'd you get hurt?"

Bounder whimpered and went left.

Jack came up behind her.

Dutch started to approach on Bounder's other side.

Caroline got as close as she dared, then dropped to her knees. She held her arms open wide. "Come on, sweetie. Come see me. Let me help you."

Bounder hesitated.

Jack caught the golden retriever in his arms.

The family pet whimpered and tried to break free. Caroline closed in, bent down to look. "It's the right front paw. Easy, girl. Easy." Gently, Caroline inspected the still-oozing wound. "It looks like she ripped off part of one toe-pad on something. I don't know if they can stitch this but she is going to have to see the emergency vet."

Dutch handed them a towel.

Bounder let Caroline wrap her paw. Jack lifted the seventy-five-pound dog in his arms, and together he and Caroline moved her to his SUV.

"You know where you're going?" Caroline asked.

Jack nodded. "The emergency vet clinic is two miles from here."

Caroline sat in the back, cradling the now steadily whimpering dog in her arms. She maintained pressure on the wound with her free hand, trying not to think about how much the paw must hurt, and buried her face in the dog's fur, talking softly to her all the while.

By the time they reached the clinic, Bounder had stopped crying. Jack and Caroline moved the still-trembling animal inside. The emergency technicians promptly took over, and moved the retriever to an exam room in the back.

Finally, it seemed, there was nothing to do but wait.

Jack filled out the paperwork, while Caroline paced.

Finished, he came over.

He looked as overwhelmed with emotion as she felt.

Caroline was already near tears. "Bounder's going to be okay, you know," she said thickly.

He nodded, his eyes moist. "I know. It's just…" He paused, for a second unable to go on. Swallowed. "Maddie loves Bounder so much. That pup is the sibling Maddie never had, and if anything were ever to happen to her…" He shook his head.

Caroline touched his arm. "Maddie would be devastated."

Jack nodded.

"So you do have a heart after all," Caroline teased, afraid if she didn't do something to break the spell, she'd be the one to take him into her arms this time.

And she had no business even thinking of comforting him that way.

One corner of Jack's mouth crooked up. "That's the rumor."

Their eyes locked. Understanding flowed. Along with the realization that the two of them made a pretty good team.

Now, Caroline thought, if they could just transfer that ability to Patrice and Dutch's wedding, they'd be all set.

It was nearly nine-thirty, but Maddie was waiting up for them when Jack and Caroline returned home, Bounder in tow.

Caroline held the leash, while Jack lifted Bounder to the ground. Together, they walked a limping Bounder over to the grass to take care of business, and then through the front door.

Inside, they were met by all three family members, and the anxious, empathetic look on all their faces let Caroline know this family had more than enough love to give.

"Is Bounder going to be all right?" Maddie asked Jack and Caroline, her lower lip trembling.

Jack bent down to unsnap the leash, then reached over and patted his daughter's shoulder. "Yes, she is." Jack had already relayed that information via a phone call from the vet clinic, but it was clear Maddie was still up because she had needed to see Bounder for herself.

The four adults watched as Maddie knelt down to greet

her beloved pet. The two went eye to eye and nose to nose, the love that passed between daughter and retriever evident. "Daddy!" Maddie worried aloud and her lower lip shot out. "Bounder looks so sad!"

Jack hunkered down beside them. "That's because Bounder doesn't like her Elizabethan collar," Jack explained.

It did look a little weird, if you had never seen one before, Caroline thought. The black cushion-collar fanned out from the pet's head, like an inverted cone or a satellite dish. It was designed to keep a dog from licking or chewing a wound.

"But she has to wear it, so she won't try and take off the bandage on her paw," Caroline explained.

Maddie transferred her attention to the thick wrapping obscuring Bounder's paw. "Her bandage is purple!" Maddie admired.

Everyone grinned.

Jack went on to explain. "The vet gave Bounder medicine and said she has to rest in order to feel better. So we're going to put her to bed now, okay? And I want you to go to bed, too."

"Can she sleep on her cushion in my room?"

Jack nodded.

Maddie kissed and hugged her dad good-night, then turned to Caroline shyly. "Thank you for helping save my dog," she said. She held out her arms.

Surprised and touched by the show of emotion, Caroline knelt so they could hug. She held Maddie close, deep maternal feelings welling up inside her. "You're welcome, honey."

Maddie held on a little while longer, then reluctantly let Caroline go. She looked at Caroline's elegant business suit. Shook her head. "Your clothes are all icky. Yours, too, Daddy."

Jack wasn't sure why he hadn't noticed until then. He supposed it was because he had been so focused on Caroline's emotions—which had mirrored his—and the continued welfare of the beloved family pet, but now that he took a good look, he saw Maddie had a point. Both he and Caroline had a mixture of dog saliva, mud and dried blood staining their clothes.

Out of the mouths of babes...

"Maddie's right. You can't go anywhere looking like that," Patrice declared. "Caroline, I'll get you something to change into. Jack, get out of those clothes and bring them down to the laundry room for soaking. If we act quickly, there's a chance we can save them with some enzyme spray."

JUST AS IT HAD BEEN with her own mother, it seemed there was no arguing with Patrice once Jack's mom had her mind made up.

So, in the hopes that her elegant business suit could be saved, Caroline accepted Jack's white oxford cloth shirt, the oversize gray workout shorts and white cotton crew socks Patrice returned with. There wasn't a lot of choice. Caroline would never fit in anything the very petite Patrice had in her closet. It would have been embarrassing to try.

Better to tighten the drawstring waist on the men's shorts and head for the laundry room, where Patrice was already spritzing the stains out of Jack's clothes with an enzyme pretreater.

Patrice frowned at the silk-and-cotton fabric in Caroline's hands. "I'll give it my best effort."

"Don't worry about it, if it doesn't come out," Caroline said.

"Of course we'll worry about it," Jack said from behind her. He, too, was dressed in running shoes, shorts and a tight-fitting T-shirt that showed off his six-pack abs. "We're responsible for the state of those clothes."

"Why don't you two let me worry about the laundry," Patrice suggested, "and you two figure out what Bounder stepped on in the yard. Because whatever it is that cut her foot is still out there and I don't want Maddie running into it."

Jack plucked a big flashlight out of the built-in cabinet above the washing machine. He turned to Caroline, seemingly in no hurry to see her leave. His eyes warmed as they slowly moved over her face, before returning to her eyes. "You up for it?" he asked.

"Sure," Caroline said, wanting to do everything she could to make sure the little girl and her pet were safe from here on out. Telling herself there was nothing at all romantic in the overture—Jack was just being friendly—she shrugged. "I'm curious, too."

Jack grabbed another heavy-duty flashlight for himself, while Patrice loaned Caroline a pair of construction boots that also looked like they belonged to Jack. She paused to lace them up. Although large, they would offer excellent protection.

Jack switched on the outdoor lamps, but the circle of yellow light only went so far in the dark half-acre yard. "So how'd you get so good with dogs?" Jack asked, glancing at her appreciatively. "Have one as a kid?"

Caroline warmed at his praise. "No. I always wanted one, but my mom was allergic so I could never have one."

Jack gave her the sympathetic once-over. "That's too bad."

Caroline tingled every place his gaze had touched and every place it hadn't. "I figured I'd have one when I finished school and got married, but my fiancé didn't want one. He thought they were too much trouble. So I put my dream of owning a dog on hold again."

Still focused on the search for the mysterious sharp object, Jack edged nearer. "Why didn't you get one when you broke up?"

Their beams of light intersected and joined. Caroline shrugged off her disappointment. "I wanted to get a puppy and raise her to adulthood, and I knew I was going to be putting every spare moment into building my business." She paused, bit her lip. "It didn't seem fair to bring a dog into my life only to leave her at home alone all the time, so I let that particular dream go again."

Jack hunkered down and inspected the bushes along the back of the fence. "That's too bad." He studied her face, then said softly, "You've got a real affinity for animals."

*And you,* Caroline thought, shocked at the realization.

Glad it was too dark for Jack to pick up the blush now heating her face, Caroline turned her attention beneath a bed of flowers. "I figure I'll have a dog one day, when I get a house and yard and a family of my own." She paused to examine the underside of the plants.

Jack slid his hand beneath her elbow, steadying her as she stood upright once again. "Don't wait too long," Jack quipped.

Shimmering with awareness, Caroline slipped from his grip and turned her attention to the dark corner of the yard along the side of the house they had yet to explore. "To do what?" she asked as he came up beside her. They were standing so close she could feel the heat emanating from his powerful body.

"To do whatever you need to do to be happy," Jack said.

Happiness, Caroline thought, meant only one thing—the fulfillment of all her dreams. Especially new romantic ones coming to mind right now.

She tilted her head up to his, asked softly, "Why do you care if I am or not?" They were only consultant and client...weren't they?

Jack paused, then switched off his light. "I'm not sure why I care so much," he said finally, switching off her flashlight, as well. "I just do. And believe me," he finished ever so quietly, ever so purposefully, "that's a surprise to me, too."

The way he looked at her made her catch her breath. "Jack..."

Her whispered plea did nothing to stop him.

Jack cupped her trembling shoulders between his palms. Slowly tilted and lowered his head, until she was awash with sensation and his mouth was a fraction of an inch above hers.

"I've got to kiss you, Caroline," Jack murmured.

And he did.

CAROLINE THOUGHT—or was it just hoped?—she had imagined how wonderful Jack's kiss had been. She hadn't. His kiss was pure heaven, and so was the feeling of being held in his arms. She couldn't say why exactly, she just knew that as his lips molded themselves to hers, eliciting tingles of heat, she felt cherished and protected, admired and desired, in a way she never had before. She felt very much a woman to Jack's man, and that was why, for both their sakes, it had to stop.

Jack felt Caroline's hesitation in the sudden stillness of her slender body and the catch in her breath. If he were smart, he would heed the signal and pull away, because making out like this in the dark was not something either of them should be doing. But common sense had little to do with his feelings at the moment.

He wanted Caroline in a way he had never desired any woman. He wanted to taste the sweetness of her lips, and feel the soft curves of her body pressed up against his. He wanted to savor the feel of her arms wrapped around his neck, the intimacy of her fingers sliding through his hair, the feel of their bare legs pressing together. The fact she was wearing his clothes at the moment only made the clinch sexier.

Kissing her like this made him feel alive. Made him want the kind of closeness he thought had passed him over.

There was just something between them. Something indefinable but definitely there. Call it a spark of awareness, the engineer in Jack thought. Dub it chemistry or the flash of opposites attracting.

All he knew for certain was that he and Caroline were different in so many ways. And yet pulled toward each other, too.

To the point her reticence had once again faded and they were making out like a couple of teenagers, both of them loving every single second of it.

And that was, of course, when the sound of the sliding door to the patio could be heard opening and closing. "Jack! Caroline!" Patrice called out to them. "What on earth are you two doing?"

# Chapter Six

Jack and Caroline broke apart like a couple of guilty schoolkids. He had only to look at Caroline's face to realize how mortified she was, and how deeply satisfied he felt.

He couldn't blame her. They were behaving recklessly. And neither of them were reckless people. Which made this incident all the more profound, in his opinion.

Jack picked up the flashlights from where they had fallen on the grass and switched them on. He handed her one and slid his hand beneath Caroline's elbow. Then escorted her around the side of the house, where they could now see his mother standing perplexed on the stone patio.

"Did you find what might have cut Bounder's foot yet?" she asked.

Jack shook his head. He looked at Caroline, saw she appeared equally unsettled. The knowledge only deepened his pleasure. Maybe they were on to something here, although he doubted it was true love. True love, from what he had been able to tell and experience, did not really exist except in movies, books and the minds of those willing to substitute emotion for cold, hard fact.

Aware his mother was looking at them with a smile now, Jack felt a stab of self-consciousness.

"Mmm-hmm." Patrice folded her arms in front of her,

the way all moms did when they suddenly caught on to something. "I can see how hard you're working."

Guilt flooded Jack. He hadn't meant to clue anyone else in on his attraction to Caroline. At least not at this point. "We'll find it," Jack promised, forcing himself to get back on task. They had no choice. The yard would not be safe to play in until they did.

Patrice continued to study them, then sobered, forcing herself to get back to the matter at hand, too. "Maddie told me she thought that Bounder hurt her foot somewhere near the slide on the swing set, if that helps."

It did. "Thanks, Mom," Jack said.

He headed over in that direction, Caroline right beside him. Patrice went back inside the house.

Carefully, Jack focused his yellow beam on the thick layer of cedar chips beneath the elaborate wooden swing set and climbing fort. "Sorry about that," he told Caroline. It was obvious that although his mother hadn't actually seen them kissing, she had figured out the gist of what had been going on between him and Caroline. And more, looked happy for it.

Unfortunately, Jack couldn't say the same about Caroline.

Head bent, Caroline studied the area around the swings. "Sorry for the kiss?" She enunciated clearly, letting him know she did not appreciate his timing. "Or the fact you embarrassed me in front of a client?"

Jack knew she was right—here and now had not been the time to make a move. He should have waited, he admitted ruefully, until there had been zero possibility of a private moment turning into a public display of affection. Next time, he'd use better judgment. He leaned closer and said, just as quietly, "Trust me. If Mom blames anyone for the fact we were making out just now, she blames me."

Jack watched the sparks come into her pretty eyes.

She tilted her head, mocked him with a glance. "You hit on the hired help that often, hmm?"

It was all Jack could do not to haul her into his arms and kiss her again, just to show her he meant it. And she had, too. Jack clamped a hand on her shoulder and guided her all the way upright. "First of all, I don't consider you part of the hired help. You're a professional, just like me. We're completely equal in that regard. And furthermore, you know it. Second, I agree my timing could be a lot better."

"It still can't happen again," she stipulated, just as firmly.

Given the fact that he had acted impulsively twice around her, and she had surrendered to the free-flowing desire between them just as easily, Jack wasn't going to make any guarantees about not putting the moves on her again. And he didn't think she should, either.

He dropped his hand to his side. "I don't make pledges I know I can't keep."

"OH, MY WORD! Is that what Bounder cut her foot on?" Patrice gasped, half an hour and a great deal of searching later.

Jack held up the three-inch chunk of cedar with the razor-sharp edge to show his mother and Dutch. "It was buried halfway down in the layer of mulch. It must have been there all along. Probably just didn't get chopped up to begin with."

"I'll call the landscape company first thing, let them know what happened, and have it all removed."

"We didn't see anything else," Jack said. And once they located the problem, he and Caroline had both used heavy-duty gardening gloves and small rakes to conduct the search. "But it's a good idea, just to be sure. Meantime, I'm going to talk to Grady. I know he recently had some sort of soft-surface material put beneath the swing set in his yard. Maybe that's the way to go. Temporarily, we can have some sod put in around the play equipment."

Patrice nodded in agreement, then looked at Caroline. "Good news. I was able to get the stains out of your clothes. But you'll probably want to have it dry-cleaned. And I would be happy to do that for you…"

"No, that's fine," Caroline interrupted with a smile. "I'll just change and be on my way."

"Also, your cell phone went off several times."

Caroline retrieved her purse and cell phone. All business, she scrolled through the messages. "It was Jericho. He wants to reschedule for seven-thirty tomorrow morning, here at the house." She looked Jack square in the eye.

Clearly, she was still a little ticked off at him for refusing to promise not to kiss her again. Not that there would have been any point in that. They both knew, given the heat of the sparks between them, it was bound to happen again. And again…

"Can you handle eating cake that early?" she asked.

In truth? Jack could handle anything that involved spending time with Caroline. "Sure," he vowed.

Caroline turned to Patrice and Dutch. "Jericho understands you can't have a lot of rich food, but he'd really like you to taste the final selection before the order is made. So if you wouldn't mind being here, too…?"

"No problem," Dutch and Patrice said in unison.

And just that suddenly, Jack noted, the event turned into a family affair.

"DADDY, I CAN'T GO to school when Bounder is wearing her E-collar," Maddie told Jack at the conclusion of the cake tasting and ordering the next morning.

Caroline paused in the act of helping Jericho clean up the last of the doily-covered paper plates. Jack's daughter was wearing a rainbow-colored, polka-dotted shorts-and-top set, suitable for the warm spring weather, athletic socks and high-top sneakers. Her cheeks were pink with agitation, her eyes shimmering with emotion. Her dark hair had been brushed into a smooth, shiny cap that swung forward to curve against her chin. She was a seven-year-old hell-bent on protecting her beloved pet, and she looked adorable.

Maddie fingered the dog's E-collar. The cushioned black fabric had been decorated with colorful stickers that kept falling off.

Caroline could see Maddie's frustration over that, too.

Maddie glanced at Jack and pouted. "Bounder looks so sad, Daddy! Like she needs me to be here with her!"

Jack barely looked up from the screen of his Black-Berry as he scrolled through the messages that had come in during the cake testing. Finally, he looked up, appearing the picture of the distracted, somewhat harried-working single dad. A look that Caroline also found adorable.

Jack put his phone aside and knelt down to talk to Maddie on her level. "Honey, I am sure Bounder will be fine. She'll probably fall asleep the moment you walk out the door, the way she does every day after you leave for school." The matter apparently closed, as far as he was concerned, Jack stood.

Unconvinced, Maddie got down on her tummy and lay so she was face-to-face with her beloved pet. The two of them went nose to nose, with Bounder staring with a mixture of mournfulness and love into Maddie's big eyes. "See, Daddy, she is begging me to stay because she doesn't want to be alone!" Maddie complained.

Jack looked at his mother for help.

"Honey, normally I would stick to Bounder like glue, but Dutch and I are going to Houston this morning."

Jack did a double take.

Apparently, Caroline noted, this was the first time Jack was hearing about that. He wasn't particularly pleased.

"For the weekend?" he asked.

Today was Friday.

Patrice shook her head—a definitive no. Dutch said nothing. "We'll be back this evening," she promised.

Maddie tugged on Patrice's blouse. "Can't you go another time, Gram?"

"Maybe over the weekend or early next week?" Jack suggested.

Patrice didn't even look at Dutch, she simply shook her head. "No, darling, we can't. I'm sorry. We have to go."

Jack continued to look at his mother with that same inscrutable look.

"We're meeting someone this afternoon," Patrice said in a clipped voice that, although pleasant, indicated annoyance at Jack's third degree. "So we really have to go if we're going to catch our flight."

Finally, Caroline noted, Jack spoke up. "Business?" he inquired almost too casually.

"It's personal," Patrice said, averting her glance as if suddenly unable to meet her son's eyes.

"I have someone I have to see," Dutch said vaguely. And left it at that.

Goodbyes were said. Patrice and Dutch rushed out the door, with only her handbag and his car keys and wallet in tow.

"Well, I better get a move on, too." Jericho gathered up his order notebook and portfolio of designs, leaving a few of the cake samples he'd brought with him on the table. "Thanks for the business," he told Jack.

Jack nodded. "Thanks for accommodating us after last night's crisis."

Jericho nodded. The door closed behind him.

Tears trembled on Maddie's lashes and she began to cry in earnest.

Jack knelt down.

"Someone has to stay with Bounder!" Maddie wailed. "We can't leave her all alone after she got hurt!"

Caroline looked at the golden retriever's sad face. Her heart went out to the ailing pet, too. That piece of wood Bounder had stepped on had been terribly sharp, going right up between her toes, slicing between two of the pads of her feet. The vet had prescribed antibiotics and pain meds to be taken temporarily in addition to bandaging the paw, but it still had to hurt. Worse, there was no way to really explain to the dog that it would get better in a day or so, although the vet had said complete healing would take a good fourteen days. Until then, the golden needed a lot of tender loving care, which would be in short supply, at least for the next seven or eight hours.

Caroline knew what she had to do. "I can stay with Bounder," she volunteered.

It was hard to tell at that moment who looked more relieved. Jack or Maddie. "You sure?" Jack asked, gratitude in his voice.

Caroline nodded. "Most of what I have to get done today for your mother can be done either by phone or on my laptop. It's no problem for me to keep an eye on Bounder while I work." Caroline bent down to simultaneously comfort Maddie and gently pet her dog's fluffy golden mane. "I promise you, I'll take very good care of your puppy dog while you are at school."

Maddie thrust herself into Caroline's arms and hugged

her fiercely. "Thank you so much!" she whispered, trembling.

"You're welcome," Caroline said, hugging Maddie back.

Finally the little girl let go. Caroline stood. Found herself looking into Jack's eyes. Something unexpectedly warm and intimate passed between them. An answering thrill swept through her.

"Maddie's not the only one who is grateful," he said.

Caroline waved off his thanks self-consciously. "It's no big deal."

"Yes, it is," Jack differed softly. He reached over to briefly squeeze her hand. "And I promise, I'll find a way to make this up to you."

ANXIOUS TO SEE how things were going on the home front, Jack let himself in at lunchtime. He found Caroline seated cross-legged on the living room floor, heels off. A throw pillow served as a desk on her lap. She had a yellow pad full of notes balanced on one thigh, her laptop computer centered on the pillow. Cuddled up next to her, spine pressed against Caroline's thigh, was Bounder. Caroline was staring at the computer screen while absentmindedly petting the golden retriever.

Bounder looked at Jack. Thought about getting up and coming over, but then decided to stay where she was.

Jack couldn't blame the dog. It looked like a warm and cozy place to be.

Looking as gorgeous as ever in a crystal-blue pantsuit that matched her eyes, Caroline made a teasing face and narrowed her glance at him. "Come to relieve me? Because you didn't have to." She bragged, content, "Bounder and I have already gotten a lot done this morning."

Trying not to think how perfectly Caroline fit into his

personal life, Jack set his BlackBerry and keys on the foyer table next to the stairs. Coming home to her like this was nice. He quirked his brow. And gave her his full attention. "Such as?"

She tucked a strand of copper hair behind her ear. "We ordered the wedding invitations your mom wanted and sent the guest list and the product to the calligrapher who will be addressing them. Your mom and Dutch have yet to decide on whether they want a DJ or a band, and have asked me to get sample performances of both to look at, which I think is wise."

Figuring he couldn't go wrong where Caroline was concerned by talking business, Jack edged close enough to see the faint imprint of freckles on her cheeks. "Which do you prefer?" he asked.

A smile spread across her face. "Both have advantages. A live band is always exciting and makes the event feel special. With a DJ, we can control the sound quality a little better, and provide a good mix of tunes—oldies but goodies for your mom's set, alternative for the younger, and country for just about everyone, since it's illegal to live in Texas and not like country music." Caroline paused, meeting Jack's eyes. "It's really up to the individuals involved."

Jack grinned. "You like your job," he observed.

"Some days, yeah. It can be fun making people's dreams come true."

"And other days…?"

"Occasionally, I have a client who is a pain."

Like me, Jack thought.

She looked at the take-out sack in his hands. "What do you have there?"

Trying not to think about fulfilling his most recent wish and kissing her again, Jack set the bag down next to her. He had promised her he would pay her back for her generosity this morning, and he was. "The rumor is you are wild about Southwestern chicken salad for lunch."

Caroline peeked playfully at the plastic-topped containers. The two salads looked generous and wonderful. They were also identical. She grinned. "Does it have guacamole-ranch dressing and tortilla strips?"

Jack offered her a hand up. "You betcha."

Caroline tightened her fingers in his as she rose graciously to her feet. A tingle of awareness swept through him as soon as they were eye to eye. "That's really sweet." She flashed a grateful smile. "You didn't have to do this, though."

JACK, HOWEVER, seemed to think he did.

Jack picked up his bag and led her through the kitchen toward the deck. "Were you going to leave Bounder to go get lunch?"

"No." Ignoring the flush of awareness she felt at seeing him again, Caroline stepped outside. She knew this was a way to repay her kindness to his family. But to her, it had that "first date" feel…. Which was ridiculous, really, since she had declared they weren't going down that road, at least not right now. Not until the wedding was over…

"Raid our fridge?" Jack persisted.

"Uh, no." Caroline appreciated the beautiful, temperate spring day, the fact that Jack was standing right beside her.

"Then you were stuck," Jack said, opening the umbrella.

Caroline wrinkled her nose, not willing to concede the point, or allow herself to be vulnerable to him in any way. "Unless I ordered something delivered," she said back, maintaining a casual tone.

Jack held out her chair, paused. "Did you?"

Trying not to think how handsome Jack looked, with his dark hair gleaming in the April sunshine, Caroline took the seat offered. "I hadn't gotten around to it yet," she admitted, glad the open umbrella offered respite from the bright midday sun.

"Good." The spring breeze ruffled Jack's hair as he laid out the packets of napkin-wrapped silverware next to their plates. "Because I should have told you earlier I'd bring lunch. Would have," he amended with his innate protectiveness, "if I'd thought of it at the time."

Caroline shrugged, unwilling to admit how glad she was he had shown up to liven up her day. "You had your hands full just getting Maddie out the door."

Jack conceded ruefully, "She can be a pistol."

Caroline lifted the salads and two bottles of water out of the bag, and then set it aside. She pressed her index finger against her chin in a parody of thoughtfulness. "Hmm. I wonder who Maddie takes after," Caroline teased.

He clapped a hand to his chest, pretending to be wounded. "Surely you're not insinuating…?" He mugged comically.

Caroline grinned back. Still holding his eyes, she allowed facetiously, "Your mom *may* have told a couple stories."

Jack settled in the chair opposite her. Their knees brushed accidentally as he attempted to get comfortable, sending another wave of heat soaring through her. "Such as?"

Caroline spread her napkin on her lap. "Your quest to keep your dad working at his job as long as possible after he got sick."

Jack looked momentarily taken aback she knew that. He shrugged, as if it were no big deal. "The school district wanted to force my dad into an involuntary sick leave slash early retirement as soon as he was diagnosed with Lou Gehrig's disease. They thought he wouldn't be able to teach senior high science anymore with amyotrophic lateral sclerosis. So I rallied the student body and started petitions, and made enough of a ruckus that parents and the local press got involved. Eventually, the school board and the attorney representing the district reconsidered their initial decision, and let my dad stay in a classroom, where he continued to teach for several more years. Some of it in a wheelchair, but he loved his work."

Caroline's admiration for Jack grew. She reached across the table and gently touched Jack's arm. "And you and your mom, apparently."

Jack nodded slowly. "He was a good man who suffered more than he deserved at the end."

Caroline understood enough about the debilitating disease—which was hallmarked by a slow-moving paralysis that eventually affected speech, swallowing and breathing—to know it was devastating, not just to the patient but to everyone around them. She sent Jack a compassionate glance. "How long was he sick?"

Jack worked the top off his salad. "Eleven years."

Caroline added guacamole-ranch dressing to hers. "And you were how old when he was diagnosed?"

Jack sprinkled on the thinly sliced tortilla strips. "Fifteen. Twenty-six when he died."

Bounder came to the glass door. Jack got up and let her out so she could join them on the deck. "It must have been hard for you."

Jack's expression turned brooding. He sat back down. "It was a lot harder for my dad. My mom endured a lot, too. She really loved him and it was hard for her, seeing him suffer."

Caroline imagined that was so. "She said that was when she started her perfume business in a big way."

Jack nodded. "She had always mixed up fragrances for herself and for friends on a part-time basis, but with Dad no longer working and medical costs mounting, she had to do something that would bring in money and still allow her to be home and near him. So she started drumming up business by advertising and writing articles for newspapers and magazines."

Caroline recited what Patrice had told her. "Which in turn is how *you* got into electronics."

Jack chuckled, embarrassed by what he obviously sensed had been a glowing recitation, and ran a hand through his hair. "Mom really *has* been talking."

"What can I say?" Caroline teased. "She's proud of you and your success."

Jack chuckled. "Dad wanted to set up a laboratory for Mom in the walk-out basement of the home I grew up in, which was unfinished at the time. We didn't have the money to have it done professionally, and he couldn't help, so he talked me through the layout and instructed me on all the wiring and lighting. We added an intercom system so he could communicate with her, even when she was downstairs working."

Caroline took a bite of spicy chicken. "Sounds fascinating."

"For a kid still in college?" Jack laughed as the memories took a positive turn. "It was incredibly exciting and satisfying. Anyway, from there we moved on to installing satellite, upgrading the interior wiring, putting together computer networks, linking our home computer and my mom's business, and trying to set up a home security system, which had a ton of bugs but was eventually successful."

"And all that led to you starting your own company when you graduated from college."

"Dad helped me with that, too." Jack's mood became peaceful, reflective. "My dad was gone by the time I really became successful." Jack looked reverently toward heaven. "But I think he knows what I was eventually able to build in terms of my business because of him and all the time he gave me."

Caroline imagined that was so, since she, too, believed the spirits of loved ones lingered on. Once again, their glances held. "You really loved him."

"I really did, and do today." Jack made no effort to quash the wealth of sentiment and affection in his voice. He paused. Looked away for an emotion-filled moment. Finally, he continued in a rusty-sounding voice. "So did my mom." He sighed, shook his head. "Which is why I find her relationship with Dutch so...unexpected."

Caroline could see that this was hard for Jack. Maybe she could help. "You don't think it's possible to love twice?" she asked gently. She gave him a moment to reflect. "I mean, it sounds like she was a pretty great wife."

"She was." A pensive silence fell. Jack took a long sip of spring water. "I used to watch them together, particularly after my dad got so sick he couldn't move anything but the muscles on his face." He turned to Caroline. "There was such deep abiding love between them. I was envious." He paused again, slowly spearing a bite of salad with his fork. "I've never seen her look at Dutch like that."

Caroline knew dreams came in varying intensity and complexity. It did not make them any less potent or satisfying in the end when achieved. Once again, she reached across the table and lightly, empathetically, touched Jack's arm. "Maybe your mom doesn't feel about Dutch the way she felt about your dad. That doesn't mean she doesn't love

Dutch, or won't be happy with him." Happiness came in all forms, too.

His disapproval obvious, Jack sat back and muttered, "I can't see how, having had one great love in your life, you could ever be satisfied with anything less."

Caroline returned ruefully, "That's only a problem for people who've been lucky enough to experience that. I never have."

Jack scoffed. "Me, either."

Together, they released mutual sighs of heartfelt resignation. Which was something else, Caroline thought, they had in common.

Finally, Caroline offered one small shred of hope. "Well…maybe someday."

Finished with her lunch, Caroline stood and placed the take-out containers into the sack for disposal.

Bounder lumbered to her feet and came over to be petted. Caroline slid her hand into the center of the padded Elizabethan collar and stroked the ailing dog behind the ears, on the face, the top of the head, under the chin. Loving the attention as well as the loving ministrations, Bounder groaned in canine ecstasy.

"One can dream, anyway!" Caroline said.

Jack's eyes glittered with wry bemusement. "Or in our case, just put off inevitably," he murmured.

Sensing a thinly veiled criticism, Caroline straightened in indignation. "What's that supposed to mean?" she demanded of Jack, as Bounder regained her energy and padded down the deck steps and into the yard. She and Jack weren't the same! Not at all! She lived for dreams. He didn't appear to have any—personal ones, anyway.

Jack's eyes shuttered to half-mast. He surveyed her lazily. "You should have a dog."

Being around Bounder had shown Caroline that, too.

Not about to deny wanting what she desired, she listed all the other things she had wanted for what seemed like forever. "And a daughter and a husband and a house, and a million other things. Unfortunately, I have to be practical. And right now, I'm so focused on building my business—"

"That you can't allow yourself to dream anything for yourself that you can't control?" Jack interrupted. He stood and put his arms around her waist. Ever so smoothly, he shifted her close.

"I don't know what you mean," Caroline protested. But he thought she did.

"All your dreams—the child, the dog, the business, the house—are things that are within your control. You refuse to dream about a husband or marriage or falling in love again because those things aren't within your control, any more than they are in mine." Jack flattened a hand over her spine. Their lower bodies touched. Then their chests.

A flutter of awareness sifted through her. Caroline lifted her palms and planted them squarely on the chiseled contours of his chest. His desire for her was evident and she could feel his heart thundering beneath her fingertips. Suddenly it was hard to catch her breath. And even harder to check the hormones surging to life inside her.

"So maybe," Jack theorized with growing masculine satisfaction, "you and I aren't so different after all."

It didn't feel like they were at this moment! Upset she could be similar to him in this particular way, Caroline protested softly in the back of her throat. "Jack…"

She did not want to be vulnerable to him or to a romance that, thanks to his resolutely unromantic nature, was bound to turn out badly! But Jack felt no such compunction, apparently.

"Fortunately," Jack intoned, "this is within our power."

He grinned, all the more determined, and slowly, deliberately, lowered his head. Behaving as if he had every right to go all possessive on her, to get her interested in making love purely as a way to assuage a deep physical need, he touched his lips to hers. Contact was slow, devastating and oh, so sensual. Caroline's lips tingled. Lower still, she felt a burning desire between her thighs.

And still, Jack continued his indolent pursuit of her, sliding his fingers through her hair, kissing her lips, her cheek, her hair, and then, ever so deliberately and wantonly, her mouth again.

To the point it was almost as if he were on a mission to make her want to fulfill her own deepest wishes. To make her yearn for an intimacy that included everything but pure romantic love.

"Jack…" she said again.

He chuckled, the sound as warm and inviting as the heat emanating from his body. Still smiling, he took her hand and lifted it to his lips, kissing the sensitive underside of her wrist with his open mouth and the butterfly touch of his tongue.

"Every time we kiss, you say my name." He emitted a long, lust-filled sigh, then paused to kiss her again, deepening the evocative caress and stroking her tongue with the rough, hot velvet of his. "It's nice. Almost as nice as the way you taste. And feel."

Caroline was no stranger to the unexpected—sometimes ill-advised—couplings that invariably evolved out of someone else's nuptials. As a bridal consultant, she had seen firsthand how the excitement of the happy couple prompted everyone else to look inward. The loneliness always intensified for those not currently romantically involved.

But it was the first time *she* had been caught up in the intensity.

Ribbons of desire swept through Caroline, even as she tried to rein in her out-of-control emotions. "Is this why you came home?"

Jack cradled her cheek in the flat of his hand. Looked deep into her eyes. And kissed her hotly, thoroughly again.

"I came home to check on you," he related between subsequent caresses. "Make sure everything was all right, that the dog-sitting was going okay, that Bounder hadn't gotten into any more trouble."

She drew back, feeling vaguely irritated and a lot insulted. "I don't need to be protected, Jack." She was used to being on her own, handling whatever came her way, even when she was in unfamiliar territory. "Any more than I need to be seduced!"

He tightened his grip on her waist before she could withdraw from his arms completely, and brought her back, flush against him. The expression in his eyes was tender, respectful. He let his gaze drift over her face, lingering on her just-kissed lips, before returning with due deliberation to her eyes. "How about appreciated, then?" he coaxed softly.

So it all was just an excuse to see her and spend time alone with her, she realized.

Pretending a great deal more detachment than she felt, she resisted the intense aching need welling up within her. Then countered sternly but breathlessly, "I thought we weren't going to do this."

JACK HAD TOLD HIMSELF the same thing the first and second times they had kissed.

At the time, his rationale had made sense.

Technically, they were a good match. The two of them had great physical chemistry, and even more important, an ease in communicating with each other that was rare. He enjoyed spending time with her because she had a way of making even the most mundane things interesting and fun. She had quickly bonded with every member of his family and she fit in his life. All those things were in their favor.

Emotionally, however, Caroline was correct. They were *not* well paired. He couldn't begin to dream about the future. All he wanted to do was live in the present. Whereas Caroline wagered everything on a someday that might never come.

Hence, if they waited for the right time and the right place and the right words to make it all seem destined... well, neither one of them was probably ever going to be happy.

So it made sense, to Jack's way of thinking, anyway, to quit dancing around the inevitable and cut to the chase.

"I thought so, too." Jack shrugged, recognizing the fact he was not going to be able to give Caroline what she wanted and needed over the long haul, but knowing he could make her feel very good today, if she let him. He looked at her steadily, then continued meaningfully. "Fortunately, decisions can be rescinded, if they are the wrong ones. *If* you're game."

"Once." Tempestuous need glimmered in her eyes as she threaded her fingers through his hair and pressed her body to his in one long, electrified line. He allowed her to direct his mouth to hers. "We'll do this once." She kissed him deeply.

As their lips fused, Jack's body ignited.

He wanted her to surrender to this, heart and soul, and

he could feel her melting against him. "Once sounds very good."

Determined to make this lovemaking more memorable than either of them had ever had, Jack guided her into his house and backed her up against the wall so his hips pressed into hers. There was no mistake about what either of them wanted to happen next. She moaned as he rained kisses across her cheek, behind her ear, down the slope of her neck, before zeroing in on her mouth once again.

Caroline surged up against him and her lips parted beneath the pressure of his. Savoring everything about this day, he delighted in the sweet, warm taste of her.

Heart pounding, he took her upstairs to his bed. Watched as she undressed—quietly, deliberately—then did the same. They drank in the sight of each other. Knowing he couldn't wait any longer, had to make her his, Jack drew her onto the bed.

Caroline wrapped her arms around him and shifted so she was on top. "This feels…"

Jack cupped the weight of her breasts in his hands, brushed his fingers across the nipples, followed that with his lips. Great, he thought.

"…illicit…." Caroline gasped.

"And then some," Jack moaned as his own body hardened and pulsed, and together, they took on new heat. "If you mean that in a sexy, dangerously exciting way."

Caroline chuckled her assent and assured him, "Oh, I do."

"Then we're definitely heading into forbidden territory," he said, flashing her an equally wicked grin. *And it felt better than anything he could have imagined….*

Her lips softened beneath his and she clung to him, her fingers digging into his shoulders, his back, his hips as she passionately returned his fevered kisses. She was trembling with excitement. And so was he.

Wanting her to have everything she deserved, Jack kissed her until his heartbeat hammered in his ears and he was so aroused he could barely think. Until both of them were brimming with an emotion neither made any effort to hide. Able to feel how much she wanted and needed him, he took control and shifted positions so she was beneath him. His gaze locked with hers, he slid between her thighs, pulled her legs to his waist, and set about exploring even more.

Caroline's head fell back as she gave herself over to his tender ministrations. And only when she was wet and aching for him, did he slide her up to a half-sitting position on the pillows.

She ran her hands over the muscles of his back, his hips. Finding the hardest, hottest part of him, slowly stroking and learning. Excitement built inside him and sensations swirled. He kissed her again as her thighs fell even farther apart, over and over, until they were both lost in a frenzy of wanting. He sheathed himself with her help. Gently, tenderly, he eased the way, engaging her completely, making sure she was as ready as he. She yielded to him as if she had always been meant to be his. Her back arched and she cried out. He smiled in triumph and brought her closer yet, luxuriating in the soft, silky feel of her as their bodies merged.

Aware he'd never gotten so close to anyone so fast, Jack held her tight and urged her on with his body. Their pleasure building, plunging her over the edge, she met him wantonly, stroke for stroke, kiss for kiss. Until there was no more waiting, satisfaction rushed through her yet again, and he followed, claiming her as his.

They lay together afterward. Aware his weight was

likely too much for her, Jack rolled onto his back, taking Caroline with him.

Content to snuggle, Caroline pressed one of her thighs between the two of his, and rested her head on his shoulder.

Eventually, a trembling sigh escaped her lips. She lifted her head.

"I can't believe I just made love to someone I'm not in love with. And enjoyed it *more* than I ever enjoyed making love to someone I *was* in love with."

Jack chuckled and narrowed his eyes, for comic effect. "That is one convoluted sentence, lady."

"Thank you." Caroline straightened and preened.

He grinned at her clowning around. Figuring total honesty was the only way to deal with a situation like this, he forced himself to be candid, too. "What's even more amazing is that I know precisely what you mean. Because I feel the same way."

Their eyes met, held. Electricity, even more potent than their lovemaking, zigzagged between them.

"Like this was fun," Caroline conceded breathlessly.

As if, Jack noted, she was glad he was on the same page, and wasn't about to make more of this than there was.

"And will be fun again," Jack predicted confidently.

JACK WAS CERTAINLY presuming a lot, Caroline thought, given that she had only agreed to a fling, thus far. But why pretend that she didn't want that, too? At least on the kind of ultracasual basis she had never before indulged in.

"Sounds good to me," she murmured contentedly.

Why not enjoy herself a little until her very own Mr. Right came along? If he ever came along. As long as nothing else in her very well-ordered life was disturbed.

Hanging on to a thread of common sense, however,

she forced herself to stipulate, "But I'm going to take a raincheck until after the wedding."

Jack appeared frustrated with her demand, but not all that surprised she had made it. Another plus in his favor, Caroline thought. He could read her like a book.

"Afraid I'm going to be too much of a distraction?" he drawled.

Way too much of one, Caroline mused as she reviewed the number of things left undone.

Reminding herself that this wedding could still make or break her professional reputation, she wrinkled her nose at him, chiding, "You already are. I should have finished the workup on the possible menu selections for pricing with the caterer, nailed down the number of tents we were going to need and viewed the DVDs of the traditional dancers and strolling musicians." None of which she'd had time to do, she'd been so busy dallying with Jack and remembering what it was like to feel like a woman instead of just a workaholic.

Jack traced the sprinkling of copper freckles across her breasts. "And I should be leaving soon to pick Maddie up from school…."

Caroline knew where this was going!

She removed his hand before it edged beneath the sheet and she got deliciously sidetracked again. "Which is exactly why I have to go as soon as you get back," she said firmly.

His eyes darkened seductively. "Or not."

How easy it would be to fall under Jack's spell, Caroline mused. To let herself live only in the moment she was in, and feel joy without repercussions for the first time in a very long time. Instead of always, *always* ignoring her need for a personal life, too, and pushing on to the next goal. All to keep her heart from being broken again.

Unfortunately, as much as Caroline wished she could open herself up to love, she knew unless she could somehow receive a rock-solid guarantee that she could trust in a man and in love the way she needed to trust, that it was merely wishful thinking. There would always be a guard around her emotions as insurance, so she would never feel the pain of a failed relationship and dashed dreams again.

Aware Jack was still waiting for her to change her mind, Caroline looked him in the eye. She promised herself she was doing the right thing for all of them by putting on the brakes—for now, anyway.

"Seriously, Jack? I'll stay until Maddie walks in the door and knows that Bounder was cared for all day by me, as promised. But after that," she insisted, "it's right back to the office for me."

## Chapter Seven

Jack had just walked out the door when Caroline's cell phone rang.

"How are things going?" Patrice asked. "Is Bounder still doing okay?"

Caroline eyed the golden retriever curled on the cushioned dog bed in the corner of the living room. "She's fine. She's been sleeping on her dog bed all afternoon."

"And the wedding plans? Are you making a lot of progress on those?" Patrice asked with more interest than she had shown thus far.

"Not as much as I had hoped today," Caroline admitted, silently berating herself. She and Jack really should have waited to make love to each other until she was no longer working on Patrice and Dutch's wedding. But the temptation had been too much to resist for either of them. Which was what came, she figured, when a person went as long as they both had without hooking up. The drought left a person vulnerable in ways she sensed neither she nor Jack had expected. But it had still been fun, and she couldn't say she regretted the passionate tumble between the sheets with the handsome entrepreneur. She felt more alive…more a woman…more optimistic about everything…than she ever had. Turning her thoughts back to business, Caroline reassured Patrice, "But not to worry—I'm going to be working on them all weekend, so I'm sure by Monday we'll have the majority of the contracts for vendors in place."

"That's wonderful, dear." Patrice sighed in relief. "Dutch and I really *need* to be…" She stopped, then tried again, more succinctly. "We really *want* to be married as soon as possible."

It almost sounded like a shotgun wedding was in the works! Knowing that wasn't possible, Caroline grinned and drew on her expertise. She had a lot of experience soothing frazzled brides of all ages and personality types. "Not to worry. It's going to happen."

Patrice exhaled audibly. "Good." Her voice resonated with cheer. "Now, for why I called you. I wanted you to give Jack a message for me."

This was odd, Caroline thought, since she'd never seen Jack without his phone. Curious, she asked, "You can't reach him on his cell?"

"I hate to bother him during the workday, dear. And really, this will be easier. Just let him know that Dutch and I won't be home this evening, after all. We're going to be staying in Houston through Monday or Tuesday. And we'll be incommunicado during a lot of that time, so if you need us, just text me or leave a message on my voice mail, and I'll get back to you as soon as I can."

This was even stranger! "You didn't take any luggage."

Patrice chuckled. "I know, dear. But we'll be fine. They have stores here, too, you know. Give my love to Maddie and Bounder, and good luck with Jack. I'm sort of leaving him in the lurch this weekend, so he will likely not be too pleased with me."

Caroline hung up, and a moment later Jack walked in the door, a deliriously worried Maddie at his side. The girl ran straight for her injured dog, plopping down on the floor next to her. "Bounder, I missed you so much! I thought school would never be over so I could get home and see if you are okay." Maddie slid her face inside the inverted cone-shaped E-collar and pressed her cheek against Bounder's. The golden retriever panted happily and made a little murmur of contentment.

"Your mother called," Caroline said, suddenly not in as much a hurry to leave Jack and his daughter and their beloved pet as she knew she should be. "She said she and Dutch won't be home tonight."

Braving Jack's frown of disappointment, Caroline relayed the rest of the message from Patrice.

Jack was as displeased as Caroline had expected. "Why didn't she call me?"

Good question, Caroline thought. One Patrice hadn't answered sufficiently. "Your mother said she didn't want to bother you at work."

Jack muttered something beneath his breath that succinctly summed up his skepticism about that. His brows drew together. "Something is going on."

Caroline kind of thought so, too. Still, she felt compelled for all their sakes to offer the opposing view, in an effort to be fair. "Maybe they want some time alone."

Jack rubbed at the tense muscles in the back of his neck. "Then they would have said so."

Caroline shrugged. "Maybe it just occurred to them. People do act impulsively sometimes, you know. In fact—" she paused and gave him a telling look "—I can think of an example right here today...."

"There's a difference. I don't have designs on your money."

"With good reason," Caroline countered facetiously, in an effort to lighten his cynical mood. "I don't really have any." Every cent she made she poured right back into her business. "And since Dutch is apparently as wealthy as your mother in his own right…"

Jack scowled. "Unless Dutch has leveraged his properties to the hilt, or blew his savings in the recent downturn in the stock market. Then, for all we know, he could be teetering on the edge of bankruptcy—"

"Even if he were," Caroline interrupted, "which seems doubtful, the prenup…"

Jack paced. "Hasn't been read yet. We don't know what it says."

Caroline folded her arms in front of her and rocked back on her heels. She looked Jack up and down, shaking her head in consternation. "It must be exhausting to be you."

Jack scrubbed a hand over his face. "What's that supposed to mean?"

"I think they even wrote a song about it once," she murmured so only Jack could hear. "'Suspicious Minds'…" Caroline made a joking attempt to hum a few bars.

Jack made no effort to draw away, even as he glowered at her. "You're a laugh riot."

He was standing so close she could see the beginnings of an evening beard, which was something she'd already felt earlier, when he'd buried his face against the delicate skin of her breasts. She flushed as the erotic memory sent another cascade of pure physical thrills soaring through her.

She stepped forward, lightly tapping the center of his chest with her index finger. "And you've got to get a grip on your cynicism if you want your mother to have the happy day she should. Seriously, Jack." Caroline looked deep into his eyes. "Not everyone who wants to marry someone with money has designs on their bank account."

"You talk a good game." Jack studied her face, and his

lips curved into a wicked smile. "Yet I don't see you putting *yourself* out there."

Caroline's brows knit together in confusion. "Wasn't that what just happened between us today?"

"Actually—" Jack gave Caroline a look that warmed her through and through "—I'm not sure what that was, which is why I am so eager to try it again and find out."

They weren't touching but it felt as if they were. "You're shameless."

He did not disagree. "So," Jack said finally, "about tonight…?"

Caroline shrugged. "I'm working," she said.

Jack grimaced. "Unfortunately, so am I. Or at least I am supposed to, but since my mother bailed on me, I have no sitter for Maddie, and with it being a Friday night…" He paused, waiting.

Caroline did a double take. "Tell me you're not asking me to babysit!" she exclaimed as Maddie came racing back in again, sliding across the smooth wood floor as if into home base.

"Is Caroline going to watch me tonight? I like that!"

Oh, no, Caroline thought, looking at Maddie's eager face. Talk about breaking hearts and long-held wishes! If only the little girl didn't want a mommy. If only she didn't want a child!

"It would just be from six-thirty to nine at the latest. I'll feed her dinner, get her ready for bed, everything before I leave." Jack looked at Caroline, desperate. "Plus I'll owe you, big-time." He reached over and squeezed her hand, then waited a prayerful moment. "So what do you say?"

I COULD GET USED TO THIS, Caroline thought, several hours later.

She had gone back to the office, returned phone calls

and finished up a few things, then rushed home to change into a pair of denim capris and a boat-necked navy-and-white three-quarter-sleeved T-shirt and flip-flops. Then it was back to Jack's.

Maddie had been waiting for her, in a pair of apple-green pajamas with an adorable dog-and-cat print. Bounder was following the little girl everywhere she went.

"I think Bounder wants her collar to come off," Maddie told Caroline the moment she walked in the door.

Caroline didn't doubt that for a minute. The satellite-dish-shaped "hat" looked like a royal pain.

"Maddie," Jack warned. "We talked about this. Bounder has to wear it so she won't chew her bandage off and start bleeding again."

Maddie's lower lip shot out. "Bounder wouldn't do that!"

Caroline knelt down so she was at eye level with the little girl. "Bounder wouldn't mean to hurt herself, Maddie. But she would. Because that's how dogs take care of their owies. They lick them. And when you lick a cut like that it usually starts bleeding again. Kind of like if you scrape your knee and it starts to get better and then you fall down again and it starts bleeding all over again. Like that."

"Oh." Maddie's expression turned solemn.

"But I know Bounder appreciates how much you love her. And what good care you are taking of her," Caroline continued.

Maddie's face lit up with enough joy to inspire a thousand smiles. "I do love her very much," she said, reaching forward to envelop Caroline in an exuberant hug.

And it would be so easy, Caroline thought, as she returned the little girl's heartfelt embrace, to love you as my very own. So easy to let you into my life...

Maddie released her hold on Caroline shyly.

Her heart bursting with unexpected affection, Caroline stood.

And looked at the other person in the room she wouldn't mind calling family....

She'd had the impression that Jack was looking fine tonight when she came in, but she hadn't had a chance to *really* look at him. Now she did. He, too, was just out of the shower. He had shaved, brushed his hair. The dark suit contrasted nicely with the marine-blue shirt and striped tie. Most intriguing of all was the cologne he wore. Cedarwood and moss combined with expensive leather and crisp sun-dried linens... The fragrance conjured up an earthy sophistication...success...a briskness that was both pure Jack, and pure spring.... She had never inhaled anything quite like it, and she knew she would never forget it. Or the specific way it fit the man who had just splashed it on his skin.

"Your mother gave that to you, didn't she?"

"Conjured up for me just this week." Jack winked. "Said it's guaranteed to attract the woman of my dreams."

Patrice was not matchmaking, Caroline reassured herself calmly. And besides, she had fallen into bed with Jack that afternoon without help of such artifice.

"I wouldn't know about that," Caroline murmured, aware her attraction to Jack was so much more than his cologne. And yet, that cologne had worked to irrevocably conjure up all sorts of sensual thoughts and images...and desires.

Jack merely smiled and looked at her as if he knew exactly what she was thinking and envisioned the same.

Realizing, however, that time and circumstance were not on their side tonight, he reluctantly unlocked their gazes and knelt down to his daughter. "You be good for Caroline. She's going to put you and Bounder in bed at eight o'clock.

And no nonsense, okay, Maddie? I want you to go to sleep. So Bounder will go to sleep. She needs lots of shut-eye to get well."

"Okay, Daddy." Maddie hugged her daddy fiercely.

Jack kissed and hugged his daughter back, then stood. He paused for a pat on the head to the dog, a long look in Caroline's eyes that promised a more intimate greeting later in private, and then he was gone.

"OKAY, WHO IS SHE?" Grady asked as soon as the dinner meeting had concluded with the group of doctors who had just agreed to lease all the last available commercial space at One Trinity River Place.

"Who's who?" Jack fit his papers into his briefcase.

"The woman who has you smiling again," Travis said.

"I know that look, too," Nate said. "I haven't seen it on your face in years."

"Thanks, guys," Jack said drily, aware he was happy, happier than he had been since he could recall.

Dan fit the architectural drawings of the just-leased offices back in the carrying case. "I'm sure we'll meet her soon enough. If you're even half in love as we all suspect, you won't be able to keep whoever she is under wraps for long."

"I'm not in love," Jack said. He wasn't that naive anymore. And didn't intend to be again.

He was in lust, however. Head over heels in lust...

"You say that now," Grady predicted with a grin.

"Yeah, yeah..." Reluctant to discuss something that wasn't meant to bear greater scrutiny, Jack said goodbye to his friends and headed out.

Traffic was light for nine o'clock Friday evening. Fifteen minutes later, he was walking in the door. Caroline was in the living room, flip-flops off, sitting cross-legged on the sofa. She was using her leather briefcase as a desk. Several notepads and pens were spread out on top of it.

Jack dropped his suit jacket over the back of a wing chair, loosened his tie and the first two buttons on his shirt. Unable to help but think what a welcoming sight Caroline made after a very long day, Jack sank into the seat kitty-corner from her, and stretched his legs out in front of him. He paused to admire her pretty feet and cranberry-red toenails. Her delicate ankles, the arch of her foot, the slender heel, were all as sexy and feminine as the rest of her.

Reluctantly, Jack forced his gaze upward. If he didn't want to chase Caroline away, he was going to have to get a handle on his desire. Otherwise, she'd end up thinking he was only interested in one thing, when it was so much more than that....

Jack cleared his throat. "Maddie and Bounder are asleep, I take it?"

With close to maternal contentment, Caroline reported, "We had fun hanging out together, and then they went to bed at eight. Both of them were very tired. Bounder was all too happy to curl up on the cushion next to Maddie's bed, and she was happy as long as her pet was near."

It sounded cozy. Jack was sorry he had missed it. "Thanks for helping me out tonight," he said sincerely.

"No problem." Caroline shut down her laptop computer. "It gave me time to get to know Maddie and get some more work done on your mother's wedding."

He wondered how to keep Caroline there, without making this seem like a really lame attempt at an unofficial date. "Did you eat dinner?" he asked casually.

Caroline nodded. "I grabbed a sandwich on my way back to my apartment to change."

Jack saw his opening and took it. "But no dessert, I'm betting."

She flashed him a flirtatious grin. "That would be correct."

"Then can I interest you in some wedding cake?"

She leaned forward to put her belongings in her briefcase, the action giving him a view of the graceful slope of her neck. "If you're talking about the samples Jericho left with you this morning—"

He watched the pink of anticipated pleasure come into her cheeks. "I am."

She beamed and followed him to the kitchen. "You're on."

Glad she had decided to stay, he set out the platter of individually wrapped samples, a carton of premium vanilla ice cream and a basket of ripe strawberries. He plucked several big fragrant Texas peaches out of the serving bowl on the breakfast table. "So what did you get done tonight?"

Caroline settled on a stool opposite him. "I figured out the number and size of the tents we're going to need, and arranged for them to be delivered and set up the day before the wedding. I also ordered the mobile restrooms and the dance floor and setup."

Jack plucked the paring knife out of the block. "It seems like a lot of trouble to go to."

Caroline rested her elbow on the marble counter and propped her chin on her upraised hand. "I'm guessing if you were the one getting married you'd go the church and country club reception route."

The smell of sugary cake and fragrant peach filled the air. "Actually, I'd prefer to get married in a judge's chamber this time around if I ever do get married again, which is doubtful."

Caroline accepted the bite of juicy peach he offered.

"Why a judge's chamber? Because it would be quick and easy?"

Jack savored a bite of the tart, sweet fruit before he finally allowed, "More like somber and official." He went back to slicing up peach, arranging them on two stoneware dessert plates, then added two scoops of vanilla bean ice cream. "I'd want us both to be reminded that marriage is a binding legal contract. Getting married in a romantic venue makes it seem more fairy tale than reality, and that's not helpful in the long run."

Caroline favored Jack with a comically reproving look. "Good thing your divorce didn't make you cynical."

Jack circled the counter to take a stool right next to her. "I know I've taken off my rose-colored glasses. I think that's a good thing." He swiveled toward her. "What about you?" He brought the platter of cake samples closer. "Where would you get married?"

Caroline studied the array of tempting treats, finally settling on a slice of white chocolate cake with vanilla buttercream frosting. "Well, first of all, I think I am every bit as unlikely to get married as you are. Since I, too, do not want to have my hopes and dreams dashed ever again. But, let's say I someday meet someone so incredibly wonderful and perfect, and manage to surpass all that, and say yes to my Mr. Right's proposal. I would want to get married on a private stretch of beach at sunset in a very small, very intimate, deeply romantic and love-filled ceremony. Given my luck so far in the romance department, which is nil, I'm not likely to ever have that particular dream come true. But I have to tell you…if I ever were ready to take that leap, I would definitely want to do it with my ideals intact."

Jack mulled that over as he savored a bite of almond cake with vanilla almond icing. "I guess that, although my approach is certainly different, I would want to marry with my ideals intact, too. With such profound love and trust that I would know in my heart and my head that the union would last forever and withstand anything."

She nudged his thigh briefly with her knee. "And here I thought you didn't have a romantic bone in your body," she declared.

He grinned. The home phone rang. Resenting the interruption, Jack glanced over and saw the caller ID flash Private Number. With a raised brow, he lifted the phone to his ear, identified the voice and said, "Hey, Laura, what's up?"

When she told him, Jack groaned. "Yeah, I'm sorry," he said sincerely, irked at his own irresponsibility. "I completely forgot I was supposed to meet you downtown tonight."

JACK'S WORDS REVERBERATED in Caroline's head like a silent alarm.

*He'd been sitting here with her when he had an engagement of some sort with another woman downtown?* Jack's voice faded as Caroline walked into the living room, found her flip-flops and slid them on. Just because they'd made love recklessly earlier today did not mean they were exclusive, or might be in the future. And now that their lovemaking had gotten him back in the game...so to speak... who knew how many women were lined up, waiting to be bedded? She'd been sitting here, acting like they were on their way to becoming a couple, just because they'd hit the sheets. How presumptuous was that? Betrayal—especially from an intimate—could come when you least expected it.

Jack's voice sounded behind her. "She's coming here. And I'd like you to stay."

His audacity knew no bounds. Caroline picked up her

carryall-style briefcase and slung it over her shoulder. "Funny, I never figured you for the kinky type."

Jack merely frowned at Caroline's attempt at a joke. "Laura's a private investigator. I hired her to check out Dutch."

Relief warred with the disappointment inside her. She had thought—hoped, anyway—that Jack had seen how fruitless and wrong it was and given up on trying to delay his mother's nuptials to Dutch.

Caroline set her briefcase back down and propped her hands on her hips. She angled her chin at him, asked incredulously, "And that info is supposed to make me respect you more?"

The frown lines on either side of Jack's mouth deepened. "It's supposed to let you know that I trust you enough to allow you to hear what Laura has to say."

She liked the idea Jack trusted her. She did not like that she was now being put in a position where she betrayed Patrice's and Dutch's trust, both of whom had shown her nothing but kindness. Not to mention what it would do to her professional reputation if word ever got out she'd had anything at all to do with Jack's activities behind the scenes. "I really don't want to be in the middle of a family contretemps."

He appeared just as disappointed in her, as she was in him. "Aren't you the least bit concerned that you might be helping my mother arrange her downfall via an ill-advised dream wedding to a smooth-talking scoundrel?"

The doorbell rang. "That was fast."

Jack shrugged. "Laura was just around the corner when she called." He gave her a steady, assessing look. "So. Are you going to go? Or stay?"

## Chapter Eight

It was a test, Jack knew, and one he hadn't expected to give. But now that the moment was here, he had to discover the truth about who Caroline was. Because if Caroline could ignore the danger signs facing another woman in order to pursue her own goals, if Caroline could do everything possible to lead that other woman to the brink of financial and emotional disaster without a second thought, then she wasn't the woman for him.

Caroline studied Jack as the doorbell rang again.

"I'll stay," she said finally. "But only because I want to see and hear you proved wrong about all this."

Jack wished that would be the case. Every instinct he had told him otherwise. Dutch was concealing something. And that secret was motivating the rush wedding. Up until now, Jack had thought, or hoped, his mother had been completely in the dark. The fact his mom had relayed a message through Caroline today regarding her absence indicated she wanted to avoid direct questions from Jack. And that was not like her.

Of course, until now his mother had not had anything to hide, either, Jack realized. With a frown, Jack introduced Caroline to the private investigator while the two women sized each other up. Although they were both about the same age and successful professionals, neither looked happy about the other's presence.

"You sure you want to do this in front of Caroline?" Laura Tillman asked.

Jack locked eyes with Caroline. "She's aware of my suspicions regarding the situation," he said.

"Okay, then." Laura sat down in a chair and opened up the file in her lap. "It was my understanding that since Dutch has been in Fort Worth that he has been residing here with you and your daughter and your mother. Is that correct?"

Jack nodded.

Laura continued consulting her notes. "He hasn't stayed anywhere else?"

Jack tensed, not sure where this was leading. "No. Not a single night."

"Were you or your mother aware he had leased a furnished one-bedroom unit in Trinity Towers, the luxury high-rise apartment building just off Sundance Square, for the entire two months you indicated that he has been in Fort Worth?"

Jack's gut sank. He had expected something like this, when he'd accidentally overheard Dutch leaving a message for another woman over the phone. "Is he having an affair?"

"That, I don't know. There's no doorman. And most of the tenants are young professionals who work elsewhere during the day, and party late into the night."

This, Jack thought, did not sound good. "What about my mother?" he asked tersely.

Laura relayed reluctantly, "Her name isn't on the lease."

"Has she been seen there?"

"Not by anyone I questioned, but again, most of the neighbors spend very little time in their residences."

"There could be a logical explanation for all this," Caroline interjected.

Laura and Jack turned to look at her. Caroline lifted an indolent hand.

"Maybe Dutch just wanted his own space. He had no idea how it would be to live here with you and your mother in the time before the wedding. It could have been a complete bust."

Instinct told Jack it wasn't that simple. "There has to be another reason why Dutch rented an apartment my mother appears not to know anything about."

"You don't know for sure she doesn't know," Caroline argued. "I'm sure you don't want to think about it, Jack, but maybe they wanted a love nest. Somewhere to have a little privacy." The kind she and Jack had had this afternoon.

Jack didn't begrudge his mother a love life.

"Or is her sex life something she would have discussed with you?"

Jack returned Caroline's wry glance. "Obviously not."

Caroline shrugged. "So maybe it was a mutual decision on their part not to tell you."

"I still think if my mother knew about the apartment, she would have mentioned it to me. So Dutch must be keeping this from her," Jack said firmly.

"So ask Dutch about it," Caroline countered impatiently.

"I wouldn't advise that," Laura cut in.

Jack and Caroline turned to look at the private detective.

"If there is an innocent explanation, and your mother and her fiancé find out you had Dutch investigated, hurt feelings and a possible rift in the family could result. If there is something shady going on, you're not going to want to give Dutch a chance to cover his tracks. You're going to want to have concrete proof before you sit down with your mother to tell her the truth."

Jack clasped his hands on the back of his neck. "The wedding is in less than three weeks."

"And that gives us *plenty* of time to discover what we need to know about whatever is going on in that apartment," Laura pointed out.

Jack trusted Laura to discover it. "What about Dutch's background? Anything come up there?"

"So far as I've been able to tell, squeaky clean. All the facts he told you about himself check out. Like your mom, he was married for nearly thirty years, lost his wife to illness, and then was single for the next decade, not dating at all until your mother came along last winter."

Jack understood the reticence that came after a long marriage. His mother hadn't dated until Dutch came along, either. "And this trip to Houston? What have you been able to find out about that?"

Jack ignored Caroline's indignant glare.

Laura consulted her notes. "Dutch and your mother had a quiet dinner this evening with a prominent nephrologist and his wife. Dutch apparently sold one of his beach houses to them a couple of years ago, and the couple is considering buying a second for investment purposes."

"So the evening—indeed the whole trip to Houston—could have been built around a simple sales pitch," Jack mused, hoping that was indeed the case.

Laura appeared to have concluded nothing yet, either way. "According to the investigator shadowing them, the conversation was, by turn, lively and serious."

Which again, Jack thought, could have simply been

Dutch turning on the charm, and then moving to discuss numbers.

Laura continued her report. "The evening ended early, with Dutch and your mother promising to see the other couple again early tomorrow. The men have plans to play golf on Sunday afternoon if weather and schedules permit. And then Dutch and your mother returned to their hotel, where they appeared to retire for the night."

That all sounded very pedestrian. So why the secrecy? Jack wondered. If they were traveling to Houston to try and sell one of Dutch's properties and then needed to stay on for the entire weekend to seal the deal, why hadn't they just said so? They were all businesspeople. Jack would have understood.

They hadn't done so, however, which meant something else—something they would prefer Jack not know—was going on there. "Did Dutch and my mother know they were being followed?" Jack felt a stab of guilt just saying that.

Laura shook her head. "Which leads me to my next question. Do you want us to continue surveillance on them for the rest of the weekend?"

Jack had never been one to waste time or money. And this, at least, appeared to be a path down a blind alley. "No. Call off the Houston operatives," Jack ordered reluctantly. "But keep looking into this Fort Worth apartment, see if you can find out why Dutch leased it, and if my mother knows about it."

"Sure thing." Laura handed over the information she had already gathered.

Jack perused it, then gave it back to her for safekeeping. He showed the detective out. He returned to find Caroline ready to depart, too.

The remote look in Caroline's eyes was not a good sign.

Jack pushed the ominous feeling aside. "You don't have to leave," he told her quietly.

"I'm afraid I do," Caroline returned.

Jack waited, knowing there was more.

Caroline shook her head. Her lips took on a sad curve. "You're in the wrong here, to continue pursuing this when you know doing so will rob your mother of any happiness she is feeling right now." She held up her hands to keep Jack from taking her into his arms. "And I can't—won't—be part of it."

"CAROLINE MIGHT BE RIGHT," Nate Hutchinson said the next morning, when Jack told him what had transpired the night before. "There could be a simple explanation for the secret apartment."

While the regular security officers stepped out to allow them privacy, Jack walked Nate through the finished command center for the security team at One Trinity River Place. He demonstrated the video feed from the exterior and interior surveillance cameras on the wall of television screens.

"Believe me, I thought about that possible scenario all night." The uncertainty had been with Jack when he went to sleep last night, and when he woke up this morning.

Jack showed Nate the electronic alert system for all the smoke and carbon monoxide detectors. "That possibility would be easier to accept if I knew more about the sale of all Dutch's real estate on South Padre Island."

Nate studied the similarly equipped system for the high-rise building's fire alarm and sprinkler systems. "You want me to call in favors?"

Nate's financial services company packaged commercial real estate for investment. "Public record shows nothing amiss in Dutch's dealings. Nor is there any other obvious reason for the liquidation of all his real estate assets, except for the reason he says, that he would like to completely retire from the property management business."

On one of the television monitors, Nate watched the live feed of someone using the badge reader to get into the building. "But you want me to dig a little deeper than that."

Jack nodded, the demonstration over. Everything was operational now. All that remained of what his company had contracted to Nate's company was the hookup of the phone and computer systems in Nate's financial services offices. And that would be completed in the next two weeks. "There may be something going on behind the scenes—an eminent domain fight or offshore drilling implementation, for instance—that isn't yet showing up in public records," Jack continued. "Because he is a prominent person in the area, Dutch would be among the first to know if something like that were coming down the pike, and he might want to get out before it happened and his properties all plummeted in value."

"And you would be okay with that?"

Jack hesitated. "From a business standpoint, it makes sense for Dutch to do everything he can to protect his bottom line. Morally, it's a lot more difficult to quantify. Yes, everyone has the right to protect his or her financial interests, but is it *ethical* to sell someone a property at a high price when you have obtained inside information and know it will be worth half that in a year or so?"

"It wouldn't seem right to stick anyone with that kind of loss," Nate theorized. "And if Dutch could do it to someone else, he could conceivably do it to your mother."

"That's my fear," Jack said.

"I'll make the calls and find out," Nate promised.

Jack gestured for the security officers to step back into the command center. "I appreciate it."

Jack was halfway out of the building when his cell phone rang. His pulse kicked up when he saw the caller ID screen. His spirits plummeted at the thought of having to make more decisions about something he had little interest in. "What's up?" he asked Caroline, wondering if she was still as irked with him today as she had been last night.

"I need a decision on the mariachi band, the traditional dancers, the DJ or band, and the dinner menu. Today, if possible."

Deciding not to analyze the crisp, businesslike tone of her voice, or what that might mean for the two of them, Jack looked at his watch. The last thing he wanted to do was spend his Saturday poring over meaningless details when larger problems loomed. Like how to get his mother out of this ill-advised union without hurting her feelings or her pride. "Can't you choose?" Jack asked impatiently.

Caroline responded professionally. "You may not be the one getting married, but technically, since you are footing the bill, you are the responsible party, Jack. Your name and signature have to be on all the contracts. For all our sakes, you need to be sure you are getting what you and your mother and Dutch want."

What he wanted, Jack thought, was to have met Caroline Mayer some other time, some other way, so he could pursue her the way she needed and wanted and deserved to be pursued, without all this wedding business and family drama standing between them.

"Then let's get it done," Jack said, relishing the chance to see her again, for whatever reason. "I'm downtown. Where are you?"

"My office."

"I'll be right over." Jack hung up before she could tell him no.

TEN MINUTES LATER, Jack walked into Weddings Unlimited. He was dressed in what Caroline imagined was his usual Saturday-morning attire of faded jeans, a navy pullover and running shoes. He had showered but not shaved that morning and the hint of dark beard clinging to his handsome jaw gave him a faintly piratical look. Which was not what she should be thinking, Caroline schooled herself as she ushered him into the conference room where she had set up the videos.

"No wedding to coordinate today?" Jack asked.

Caroline forced an officious smile. "Actually, I do have one this evening. My assistant is over at the hotel now, making sure everything is being set up properly for the reception."

Jack looked momentarily disappointed. Surely, Caroline thought, he hadn't been about to ask her for a date!

He glanced at his watch. "How much time do we have?"

"I have to be at the church at four." *Which meant the clock was ticking.* "So we need to get started...."

Happily, Jack was as ready to get down to business as she was. Over the next few hours, they managed to put down deposits on everything except the band or DJ. "I really am not sure which my mom and Dutch would prefer," Jack said finally.

"You'd rather wait until they get back from Houston?"

Jack nodded. Understanding, Caroline stood. "Then I'll check back with you on that early next week."

Wary of spending any more time alone with Jack, Caroline moved to quickly usher him out. For a moment she thought he would try and come up with a reason to linger. Then, after one last long look, he thanked her and left.

For the rest of the weekend and well into the next week, Caroline was remarkably adept at keeping a safe distance from the handsome man bent on delaying or halting his mother's wedding.

By Friday, however, her many excuses had worn thin, and when Patrice called demanding to see Caroline at the home she shared with her son and granddaughter, she had no choice but to honor the request.

Dutch was on his way out when Caroline arrived.

He acknowledged Caroline and hugged Patrice, who wrapped her arms around her fiancé and rested her head on his chest.

And there it was, Caroline thought, the true affection she had been waiting to see. The deep, everlasting kind that pretty much guaranteed a happy marriage.

Slowly, the older couple drew apart. "I'll be back in five or six hours," Dutch assured.

Patrice gave him another lingering glance. "I'll be waiting," she said with a blissful smile.

Bounder lay alone in the front hall, a bereft expression on her pretty golden face. The E-collar was gone and so was the bandage. Caroline knelt to pet the golden retriever. "Hey, girl," she said gently. "Your paw is looking lots better."

"It will be fully healed in another week," Patrice said. "In the meantime, she's prohibited from going on walks or indulging in any rough-and-tumble play."

"No wonder the sad expression on her face," Caroline sympathized.

"That and the fact that Maddie's still at school," Patrice said. "She's always a little blue when her best pal isn't around."

"I'll bet."

"Bounder usually waits for Maddie in the front hallway until she comes home again."

Caroline told herself she was relieved not to see Jack's

little girl. It was hard enough not getting attached to his family as it was.

"So—" Caroline gave Bounder a final pat and rose gracefully "—you said you wanted to see me to go over a few things?"

"I do," Patrice said with a regal nod of her head. "But first, I have a favor to repay. I promised you I would create a signature perfume for you. And I think it's time we got started."

PATRICE LED CAROLINE to her fragrance studio on the third floor of the Gaines home. The sunlit space featured big windows, luxurious champagne-colored carpeting and walls, and lots of glass shelving.

Patrice asked Caroline to take a seat at the counter. "We'll start by identifying the top notes that you like," Patrice said as she set out five different racks of bottled fragrances.

First up were the floral scents. Geranium, chamomile, gardenia and marigold. Caroline rated them on a scale of one to ten, liking geranium the most.

Patrice took notes on the selections, then got out another rack of top notes in the fruity class, for Caroline's perusal. "So what did my son do last weekend to drive you away?"

Caroline paused in mid-sniff.

Patrice cut her off before Caroline could voice a denial. "Obviously something, since neither he nor I have seen you in person since then."

*He made love to me. And then disappointed me.* Which was, Caroline thought, the story of her life. She found the man she thought might be The One and then discovered he was not.

But this was not Patrice's problem.

She gathered her wits and gave the older woman the professionally voiced apology she deserved. "I'm sorry if you have felt slighted. I had my assistant acting as messenger because it was a more efficient use of my time. I had two weddings to coordinate last weekend, one last night and another coming up this Sunday."

Patrice absorbed that information. And didn't buy it. She handed over a sample of black currant bud. "You don't have to protect my son. I know how single-minded he can be when he is trying to protect someone. In this case, me. What I don't know is *how* he's attempting to do so at the moment. Except that, obviously, whatever he is up to somehow involves you." Patrice handed her a sample of plum. "Obviously, you're uncomfortable being put in the middle, and rightly so. Hence, I'm giving you a chance to confess to me, and get yourself out of the center of what is a very delicate family situation."

Here it was, Caroline thought, her chance to come clean and turn Jack in to the bride, simply by confirming what the bride already sensed. Doing so *might* halt Jack's sleuthing behind the scenes and save the nuptials from potential disruption. Certainly, it would bring immediate relief from the enforced duplicity for her, and end her moral dilemma, more or less by default. So why couldn't she seem to do it?

## Chapter Nine

Caroline and Patrice had just identified Caroline's favorite top notes when a blast of music wafted up from the lower floors.

"Sounds like Maddie's home." Patrice smiled.

Caroline listened a minute and identified the crooner. "She likes Tony Bennett?"

Patrice shook her head. "I love Tony Bennett. So let's just say she's listened to a lot of his albums." Downstairs the volume increased even more. "Ten to one, she's twirling around, practicing her dancing for the wedding right now."

That sounded like something she had to see, Caroline thought. Patrice obviously agreed. "Let's go downstairs, shall we?"

"Love Is Here To Stay" filling their ears, the two women descended both flights of stairs. Caroline was not prepared for what she saw. Maddie, in her usual tomboy clothing and sneakers, her baseball cap on backward, dancing with her dad the way all girls her age learned to dance, by standing on her daddy's feet.

Jack had his back to them. Maddie was holding on to him, one hand clasped in his, the other resting on his forearm. Head tilted back, she looked up at him with sweet adoration. As they circled around, the tender devotion on Jack's face was unmistakable, too.

Without warning, a lump the size of a walnut formed in Caroline's throat. In the time she had worked as a wedding planner, she had seen dozens of daughters dancing with their dads. But it had never affected her like this. For the first time, she realized what she missed—growing up without a dad. Her eyes filled with tears. Embarrassed to be so overcome with emotion in front of a client, she muttered a quick aside to Patrice and rushed out the door, to her car.

Still trying to get a hold of herself, she stopped next to her BMW, her back to the house. If only she had a tissue out here, she thought, irritated, blotting ineffectually at the moisture running down her cheeks with the pads of her fingertips. But her tissues were inside her purse, which was inside Jack's house. Ditto her car keys. So she couldn't even open up the car to pretend to get something Patrice should see!

"Now my mom really thinks I've done something to drive you away," Jack drawled.

Cringing at the astute observation and keeping her back to him, Caroline dabbed at a fresh wave of tears. She shot a look over her shoulder and saw they were alone. Which left her free to shoot back, "Besides trying to derail her wedding, you mean?"

Jack tensed. "Did you tell her I hired a P.I.?"

Another wave of emotion flooded Caroline's heart. "No," she choked out. And for the life of her, Caroline could not understand why. She and Jack had no commitment to each other, despite the fact they had made love once. Her true duty, in this and every wedding she coordinated, was to the bride and the groom. It didn't matter who was footing the bill!

Jack stepped closer. His tall body relaxed. "Good."

Trying not to notice the way his broad shoulders blocked out the sun, Caroline angled her chin at him and studied him beneath the fringe of her still-damp lashes. "That mean you've given up?" she asked hopefully.

His expression remained as implacable as the rest of him. "It means I'm waiting for all the facts to come in."

"But you've got nothing else so far?"

"No," Jack said. "But that doesn't mean nothing will come up."

Caroline knew self-confident men like Jack wanted to be proven right. But in this case, being proven correct meant hurting his mom and quashing her dreams.

"Back to why you were upset just now," Jack said.

"It really isn't important."

"It is to me."

Their gazes locked.

She still couldn't bring herself to tell him.

Jack folded his arms in front of him. "And to my mother and Maddie, who will both have my hide if they think that I made you cry."

Caroline sighed, rolled her eyes and gave in. No sense starting a family drama. Even as she started to speak, tears began to well. "Seeing you dancing with Maddie just now brought up some feelings I didn't expect."

Jack's expression gentled as he waited for her to collect herself and go on.

Caroline crossed her arms in front of her, too. "I always told myself it didn't matter that I didn't have a dad. My mom might have been my only parent, but she was a terrific one. I figured that having one loving parent was a lot more than some kids had. And so much better than having two disinterested ones. So it's never really bothered me. Not even during all the weddings I've planned." Aware

Jack was listening intently, Caroline gestured inanely. "Seeing the fathers walk their daughters down the aisle and make their wedding toast and have that first dance was just all part of the pomp and circumstance. I couldn't miss what I'd never had, right?" Caroline paused and bit into her quivering lower lip.

She swallowed, shrugged, briefly closed her eyes. "But then I walked down and saw you and Maddie and I don't know…" With effort, Caroline lifted her eyes to Jack's. "Seeing you with her, seeing you so tender…I realized what I'd be depriving my child of if I go the single mom route, too. And yet that is the only option open to me. So I just lost it."

Jack studied her with a look that said, *You have other options, Caroline. You just don't realize it yet.* But when he actually spoke, he said, ever so quietly, "Surely there were male influences in your life."

"Teachers. Friends of the family. Friends of my mom who occasionally stepped in when a male presence was required." Caroline compressed her lips in remembered disappointment. "It's not the same as having a dad."

Jack unfolded his arms and took her hand, prying it loose from her waist. "I see your point," he soothed, giving her fingers a squeeze. "I don't know what I would have done for Maddie if my mom hadn't been around for the girl stuff all these years."

Caroline allowed Jack to reel her in to his side. "You've been lucky to have her."

He wrapped his arms around her. "You miss your mom, too."

More tears welled. The lump was back in her throat. Allowing herself to be comforted, Caroline let her head fall to his chest. "Very much," she admitted in a low, muffled voice. Being around Patrice made her long to have a mom in her life again. Being around Maddie made her want to have a daughter.

Jack stroked her hair with all the tenderness he'd shown his daughter, and something else that felt even more potent.

Caroline drew back, sure if this embrace continued Jack would kiss her. And equally sure she couldn't let him.

Patrice walked out to join them. Jack's mother looked from one to the other, her shrewd glance missing nothing. "Everything okay out here?" she asked brightly.

That depended, Caroline thought, pushing away the vulnerability she felt whenever she was with him, on whether or not getting closer to Jack was a good or bad thing.

AN HOUR LATER, CAROLINE, Patrice and Jack were deep into a dilemma of another sort. "I just can't make a decision on this." Patrice threw up her hands after an hour spent reviewing video clips on the big-screen television in Jack's family room.

"Maybe we should start by narrowing the field to DJ or live band," Jack said, clearly exasperated his mother had not approved his top choices in either category.

"I can't without seeing these people in person first."

"Mom, the wedding is a week from tomorrow," Jack said.

"This really needs to be done ASAP," Caroline said, feeling a little desperate. "I had a hard time finding groups that didn't already have a gig that weekend. Some of the ones I just showed you may already be booked."

"Someone has to see them in person," Patrice insisted again. She looked into the adjacent family room, where Maddie and Bounder were curled up on the floor, watching an episode of *Charlie and Lola,* a British cartoon about a responsible older brother and his funny little sister. "And

I'd feel better if I had more than one opinion. So perhaps the two of you should go."

Jack looked at his mother as if she had lost her mind.

"That is completely unreasonable," he said, keeping his voice low enough so only the three of them could hear. "Since you didn't like my first choices."

"Seeing something live and in person always makes the choice easier. And if you and Caroline both agree on either a DJ or a band, then I'll know it's the right choice."

Jack had the stormy look the father of the bride usually got when his daughter was driving him to distraction.

Caroline held up a silencing palm. "Let me step outside a moment and make a few calls, see if any of them have a gig tonight or tomorrow."

Silent, Jack scrubbed a hand down his face. He looked as though he were about to lose his mind.

Patrice smiled.

Caroline stepped outside on the deck into the spring sunshine. She had just finished talking to the last person when Jack joined her. "Well?" he said, looking no less grumpy.

Given the circumstances, Caroline really couldn't blame him.

"One of the DJs has a gig tonight at a local bar, the other nothing until next Friday, the day before the wedding."

"Well then, he's out," Patrice said, joining them, too.

"The two bands have weddings tomorrow evening. We can pop into the receptions and observe."

Jack studied her as if he weren't sure if she was a saint or a glutton for punishment. "You are serious about doing this?"

"It's my job to make the bride happy." Caroline paused, then, unable to prevent herself, added lightly, "What's yours?"

WHAT WAS HIS JOB? JACK wondered. To be a good son and go along with whatever his mother wanted, no matter how ill-advised? Or to protect her from a potentially disastrous decision?

"What time is the DJ on tonight?"

"He starts at eight and goes to closing," Caroline said, copying the info for him on a piece of paper. She ripped it out of her notebook and handed it to him. "How about I meet you there at nine?"

Her handwriting was as beautiful as the rest of her. "I could pick you up," Jack offered.

Caroline declined the offer with a small shake of her head. "I'll meet you in Deep Ellum," she said and then took off.

Dutch had not returned by six, so Jack had dinner with his mother and Maddie, then showered and changed. He headed for the trendy section of Dallas, where all the young single professionals gathered, many of them looking to hook up, some for the night, some for a lifetime. Jack was no stranger to the Dallas-Fort Worth night scene. A lot of business was conducted over dinner and/or drinks. He still felt oddly out of place as he parked and headed for the bar. More like a single guy on the prowl or better yet, the Tin Man in the *Wizard of Oz*…his dancing and dating moves all creaky from disuse, the place where his heart should be, empty…and suddenly in need of filling.

Not that this was a date, or anything close, he reassured himself as he walked through the renovated warehouse district, located just three blocks east of downtown Dallas. Past the throngs of fashion-forward, trendsetting partygoers, and the clubs featuring many of the newest bands, to the eclectic bar where a thank-God-it's-Friday party was in progress.

The music of The Fray ringing in his ears, Jack made

his way through the crowd to the bar. Noting Caroline wasn't there, he ordered a beer and sat down to wait.

He'd been there less than two minutes when she walked in. She'd put her hair up in a loose, sexy updo and she looked spectacular. The clinging knee-length, cap-sleeved black cocktail dress showed off her slender curves, her black strappy heels made the most of her curvaceous legs. The pink of exertion was in her cheeks, and silky copper-colored strands fell across her forehead, her cheek, the nape of her neck. She had a single black onyx pendant nestled in the *V* of her dress, between her breasts. Matching earrings adorned her ears. Most arresting of all was the happy, purposeful way she moved.

Spotting him, she glided closer and wedged her way in next to him. "So what do you think?"

That I might very well be falling in…something, Jack thought. He wasn't sure it was love. Wasn't sure he was capable of that anymore. But there was definitely something going on here, and it was a lot stronger and more complex than compatible pheromones and simple man-woman attraction.

It was his inability to take his eyes off her whenever she was close.

His incapacity to stop thinking about her when they were apart.

The fact he wanted to kiss her all the time. And if he were honest, do more than that to make her his woman, at least from a physical standpoint.

Bottom line, he wanted her in his life. Past the wedding…

And before…

"Earth to Jack!" Caroline persisted, coming even closer. "About the DJ? What do you think?"

Jack looked up, realized another song was now playing.

"I just got here," he said. "I'm going to need to have to listen for at least half an hour, if not more, to decide whether it's thumbs-up or thumbs-down. So, as long as we're here... can I buy you a drink?"

She looked at the cold longneck in his hand. "Only if there's food to go with it."

"No problem," Jack said. He leaned forward to tell the bartender, "We'll have the mixed appetizer platter and...?" He turned to Caroline.

"A Shiner Bock, too."

Seconds later, the bartender handed Caroline a brown bottle and a frosty mug. "It'll be about fifteen minutes on the appetizers," he said.

Jack pointed to a raised table in the corner. "We'll be over there."

He escorted Caroline to the table and held out the stool, which proved to be a tad difficult for her to step up into, even after she'd set the glass and bottle down. Hand beneath her elbow, he gave her a boost. "Thanks," she said, blushing slightly.

"No problem." He removed his hand from her soft skin.

"Too bad we can't fast-forward to all the breaks in the music," Caroline joked.

Who wanted to fast-forward? Sitting across from her in a lively bar on a Friday night was exactly where he wanted to be. But not sure she wanted to hear that just yet, Jack touched his fist to his chest. "Gotta take one for the team," he joked.

She smiled.

He noticed her foot was tapping to the KT Tunstall song.

He was just about to make his first foray into small talk with her, when a couple walked up to her. Subsequent conversation made it clear that Caroline had planned their wedding, for which they were extremely grateful. As soon as they left, the appetizers arrived, but the waiter forgot napkins, plates and silverware, so Jack got up to go and get some. When he returned, a good-looking guy in a business suit was sitting opposite her. It turned out to be a friend of her ex-fiancé's, who had missed seeing Caroline and wanted to know how she was doing.

Jack felt like the third wheel on what could have loosely been considered his first date with her.

It wasn't a great feeling. And made him realize how much he wanted her to be his date for the evening.

It just wasn't going to be tonight.

"IT'LL BE EASIER if I pick you up," Jack told Caroline the next morning.

Caroline shifted the phone to her other ear.

Save-the-date e-mails and phone calls had gone out the previous week, but the formal invitations for Dutch and Patrice's wedding were being mailed today, and Caroline was working with the calligrapher to make sure everyone on the list was accounted for.

"Really—" Caroline pointed to a name where no corresponding invitation could be found "—I can drive myself to both weddings."

"The first one is at a church near Bass Hall. There's a Fort Worth Symphony concert. Parking could be at a premium."

"You have a point." Caroline stopped to consider.

Accepting a ride with Jack would give the evening an intimate feel she didn't need. It would be far more difficult than meeting him at the bar last night.

She didn't want to feel they were on a date.

Having him pick her up would make it feel like a date.

But it wasn't a date. She knew that. So did he.

And besides, there were likely to be just as many diversions at the two weddings as there had been at the bar last night. They were going to check out the music of two live bands.

They'd do that and then pick one, since Jack had—for whatever reason—decided last night that the DJ was out. And then the evening would end, and she could go back to her life, such as it was, and he could go back to his, with no complications for either of them.

So why wasn't she happier about the limits she had insisted upon? Why, if she were honest, would she have much preferred this were a date, albeit one that combined business and pleasure?

"Yes or no?" Jack said finally.

They were only being practical. It wouldn't necessarily lead to anything, Caroline told herself decidedly, taking the leap of faith. "Yes."

"There's just one thing," Jack said. "A friend of mine, Nate Hutchinson, is having a housewarming party to show off his new place, and I promised I'd drop by. His home is in the same neighborhood as the second wedding. Once we conclude our business, would you mind dropping by with me?"

"Wow," JACK SAID when he arrived to pick her up at six-thirty Saturday evening.

Wow was right, Caroline thought as she took in Jack's appearance, too. He looked so good in his dark gray suit, striped shirt and gray-and-burgundy tie, he could have stepped right out of the pages of a men's magazine. He smelled great, too. Like the signature cedarwood and leather cologne created just for him.

"That's not what you say to a business acquaintance," Caroline chided.

"Can't help it," Jack said, giving her the slow, sexy once-over. He shook his head in mute appreciation. "That dress…"

It was nice, Caroline had to admit. The off-the-shoulder crystal-blue silk sheath hugged her slender torso, hips and thighs, and stopped just above the knee. It was elegant, sexy and comfortable. She had worn it to a number of weddings and always felt very at ease.

Unfortunately, there was nothing easy about Jack's gaze.

It was smoking hot.

If she looked in his eyes much longer…they'd never leave her apartment. Promising herself she was not going to let their pheromones dictate her behavior, Caroline merely smiled and led the way out the door, and down to the lobby of her building. It didn't matter how drawn she was to him. There was business to be done tonight. And that was all she could afford to focus on.

"So this is what it feels like to crash a wedding," Jack murmured twenty minutes later when they walked into the first reception.

The couple getting married was young and lively. And so was the music. The band was playing "Shout."

Grinning, Jack took Caroline's hand in his.

Before she could protest, Jack tugged her out onto the dance floor among the other revelers, where there was nothing else to do but throw up their arms and kick up their heels along with everyone else.

Three high-energy dances later, Jack observed, "Their video didn't begin to convey the energy this band has. They're great!"

"I think so, too!" Caroline said as the two of them ducked breathlessly out of the reception hall.

"The only question is," she continued as she worked to slow her pounding pulse, "is that band too lively for Patrice and Dutch? The bride and groom need to be able to keep up with their guests on the dance floor."

"Good point," Jack said.

"The next band may be more their speed," Caroline said.

The second reception was held at a country club. The bride and groom were in their early forties, and the guests seemed much more sedate. When Jack and Caroline walked in, the band was playing "Can't Help Falling in Love."

As before, Jack eased her right out onto the dance floor. Only this time, the slow tempo of the romantic song required she put her right hand in his. Smiling down at her tenderly, Jack pressed his other hand against her spine and drew her close.

Their lower bodies weren't touching, but they might as well have been, Caroline noted, she was so acutely aware of him, so inundated with memories of the time when nothing had been between their bodies, except skin....

And of course, that was when it happened, when the band decided to play that proverbial oh, so romantic wedding song, "The Way You Look Tonight."

Caroline looked in Jack's eyes. And felt her heart melt all over again.

JACK BLAMED IT on the song, the lyrics coupled with the seductive beat. He'd been doing pretty well until then, keeping the evening light and fun. But the way Caroline looked at him just then, all soft and wanting, made him realize what they'd shared had been more than just a fling.

It might not be the right time.

Or the right circumstances.

But there was something there between them. Something real. Something worthy of being pursued. And first chance he got, he was going to go after it with all he had.

In the meantime, a decision had to be made.

"This is the band," Jack said. "I want to sign them for the wedding."

"You're in luck," Caroline said as the song ended and the band ended their set. "They're taking a break."

Fifteen minutes later, the gig was set.

Caroline and Jack left the reception and headed out into the night.

"Only one more stop to make," Jack said, now wishing he hadn't agreed to stop by Nate's housewarming, and could instead head straight for something a lot more intimate. A dinner for two. And a chance to get to know Caroline a lot better.

Instead, they got in his car and drove to Nate's new digs.

"He's doing well for himself," Caroline said drily, as Jack parked in front of a multimillion-dollar mansion in one of Fort Worth's most luxurious neighborhoods.

Jack nodded. He and his friends were all remarkably successful these days. "For him, this is just another investment," Jack said.

That was especially evident when they walked inside.

The decor had a postmodernist edge that was not Nate at all.

The guests at the party were mostly upper-crust clients of Nate's financial services firm, and business associates. Everyone seemed to be talking the finer points of investment and the current economy. Compared with the two parties they had just left—one incredibly fun and lively, the other overwhelmingly soulful and romantic—this gathering was just another day at the office.

Which was, of course, where the always-single Nate felt the most comfortable. Jack could almost see Caroline stifling a yawn.

Luckily, she quickly spied Grady's wife, Alexis, and Dan's wife, Emily. Caroline smiled. The professional matchmaker and the personal chef turned entrepreneur were both friends of hers.

Alexis waved them over. "Caroline! We want you to meet Travis's wife, Holly. She's a mural artist..."

Jack left the women and headed for the bar to get drinks for both of them. Nate appeared at his side, his expression sober. "If you've got a minute," Nate said, "we need to talk."

"Sure." Jack told the bartender to wait on the drinks. He followed Nate into the study.

"Sorry to spoil what obviously looks like a helluva romantic evening for you," Nate told Jack grimly, clapping a brotherly hand on his shoulder. "But I finally got some information on Dutch. And you're not going to like it."

## Chapter Ten

"Are you going to tell me what happened at Nate's? Or am I just going to have to guess?" Caroline asked Jack when he dropped her at her door.

Jack had barely glimpsed the interior when he'd picked her up earlier. Now, she ushered him into the apartment in the midtown high-rise. The galley-style kitchen featured white cabinets, marine-blue walls, black marble countertops and stainless steel appliances. To one side was a small dining area, with a sleek glass-topped table for four. The living area featured large windows that overlooked the city streets below, and was decorated with an overstuffed ivory sofa and chairs that nicely complemented the marine-blue walls and pine furniture.

Off one door, Jack could see a bedroom with an elegant bed, strewn with clothing. An equal number of discarded shoes decorated the floor.

Caroline caught his glance. "So I had a little trouble deciding what to wear," she told him, then moved to shut the door. She folded her arms in front of her. "You still haven't told me what's going on."

Jack debated whether to downplay the situation or confide in her. Deciding he needed a sounding board, he chose the latter. "I asked Nate to use his contacts in the South

Padre real estate investment community and see what he could find out about Dutch."

Caroline sank down into one of the overstuffed armchairs and crossed her legs at the knee. "And?"

Diverting his gaze from the spectacular view of her legs, Jack moved to sit on the sofa. "Nate found out that Dutch has been frantically trying to raise money for about six months now."

Caroline met Jack's gaze. "How much money?"

"He wants five million, cash, but would settle for four."

For a moment, Caroline looked like she had been sucker punched. She held Jack's eyes for a long time. "Why?"

Jack grimaced. "No one knows."

Caroline let out a slow breath and leaned back in her chair. "Is he a gambler?"

Jack watched the way her fingers had curled tightly over the upholstered chair. "Not that anyone knows. Nor does he have any criminal connections."

Caroline's eyes narrowed. "So it's not like he owes money to the Mob or anything."

Jack shook his head. "No. Dutch has always been a respected businessman with an ethical reputation and sound judgment."

Caroline made a face that showed she was struggling to understand the situation. "So maybe all Dutch wants to do is invest in something else."

"Which would be where my mother comes in," Jack said grimly, wishing it weren't so. He was actually beginning to like Dutch.

Color blushed Caroline's cheeks. "I don't follow."

Reluctantly, Jack reported, "My mother elected to take ten million in cash and company benefits—like life, health and disability insurance—for life instead of a much smaller signing bonus and ongoing royalties."

Caroline narrowed her gaze. "So she could...?"

"Give Dutch the four or five million in cash and fund whatever it is Dutch wants to fund," Jack retorted impatiently.

"Assuming he's able to talk her into it," Caroline countered. "Your mother is a sensible woman."

Jack wished he could feel as positive. Painful experience had taught him otherwise. "I was a sensible person, too, until I fancied myself in love and started acting on emotion instead of cool reason."

Caroline crossed her legs, cupped her joined palms over her knee, and leaned toward Jack persuasively. "First of all, Jack, I don't care what it looks like," she said softly and sincerely. "Every instinct I have tells me that Dutch is an honorable guy who cares deeply about your mother. He has already made her very happy. And in her own words, brought her back to living a full life again. Which I gather, after the heartbreak of your father's illness and death, wasn't easy."

"No, it wasn't," Jack agreed, loosening the knot of his tie and the first two buttons on his shirt. "Which is why I don't want to see her hurt again." His mother had already been hurt enough. To see her lose another spouse, for whatever reason, was more than Jack could bear.

Caroline rose gracefully and moved toward him. "Second, acting on pure emotion isn't all bad, Jack."

Hoping she wasn't about to show him out, Jack got to his feet, too. "Isn't it?"

Caroline went toe to toe with him. "No." She angled her chin at him. "It's not." Her crystal-blue eyes glittered with feeling. "And if you would just stop and think a moment..."

Jack didn't want to think. All he wanted to do was react—and put an end to anything that might hurt or in any way threaten his loved ones. Caroline was preventing that. He wrapped his arms around her waist, tugged her near. "We can't all go around doing what we want to do at any given moment," he told her gruffly.

Caroline's lips curved in a half smile. Her gaze tracked the open collar of his shirt, the loosened knot on his tie, the jacket he'd wanted to take off, but hadn't. She surveyed him thoughtfully. "Because if you were doing that right now, you'd be kissing me," Caroline surmised, surprising the hell out of him.

Jack saw no reason to lie. "That's exactly what I'd be doing."

Caroline's eyes sparkled unexpectedly. "Then let's get to it," she said.

CAROLINE TOLD HERSELF all she was doing was saving Jack, his mother and Dutch a lot of heartache, by passionately distracting Jack and keeping him from acting on his suspicions.

It had nothing to do with the fact she'd been wanting Jack all evening.

She paused, her lips just under his. She was certain if Jack would just allow himself to be vulnerable he could fall in love again, the way she was starting to fall in love.... "You're resisting," she noted, grinning flirtatiously, already rising to the challenge that was this man.

"You noticed," Jack murmured back.

It was at this point that a lesser woman would have thrown in the towel and called it a night. Let him go wreak havoc on his life with no further interference from her.

Then Caroline thought about the way he had looked at her the night before when she had walked into the bar to meet him. The fun they'd had tonight at the first wedding, when they'd hit the dance floor and really cut loose. The tender way he'd held her close at the second wedding, when they'd slow-danced to all those romantic songs. The way he'd made love to her, days ago. What a good team they made.

They might not want to admit it, but something was happening between them, and she could no more deny it than she could deny the desire welling up inside her.

If Jack were honest, she knew he would not be able to deny it, either. And if it took an event like this to prompt them to come together, then so be it. "Then I'll just have to work harder to tempt you," she whispered playfully. Going up on tiptoe, she fit her lips against his.

To her frustration, the fireworks remained muted, and the barrier between her and the tender recesses of his heart remained.

Amused at the role reversal going on here—wasn't this supposed to be his move, instead of hers?—Caroline deepened the contact by pressing her lips even more ardently against his.

Emboldened by the evidence of his desire, Caroline stepped farther into the embrace. Her breasts rubbed up against his chest, as did the rest of her from shoulder to knee. She eased the tip of her tongue along the seam of his lips. Loving the taste and feel and scent that was uniquely him.

Her pulse pounding, she caressed him from shoulder to spine, to waist, to hip, again and again and again, putting everything she'd been holding back, everything she had dared not express into the embrace, until Jack finally relented with a groan. He went from passively participating to actively pursuing in a flash, clamping his arms around her, hauling her closer still, and opening his mouth on hers.

The touch of his tongue to hers was hot, electric, mesmerizing. The enveloping heat of his body gave new urgency to hers. It no longer mattered how or why they were together like this, just that they had found reason to come together again. To talk and laugh and argue and look in one another's eyes. To know that there was so much more to life than either one of them had been experiencing....

Finally, Caroline tore her mouth from his. "Let's go to my bed...." she coaxed, spreading her hands across his shoulders, chest. *Let's get rid of the differences between us...and instead, focus on all that is right.*

His eyes darkened. He searched her face. "You're sure...?"

"Very."

Jack took her hand. Together, they went into her bedroom, where the soft lamp next to the bed had been left on. Caroline blushed when she saw the dozen dresses and matching undergarments still scattered across her bed.

"That must have been some wardrobe crisis," Jack teased as Caroline scooped up the garments and tossed them onto the upholstered bench at the foot of her bed. She knelt and swept her shoes out of the way, too.

When she rose and turned back around, Jack had his suit coat off. With one hand, he was removing his tie. Feeling more seductive than she ever had in her life, she toed off her heels. Pulse racing, she walked toward him with the rolling hips of a runway model. "Let me do that for you."

Their eyes locked and held as she put his tie aside, unbuttoned his shirt, pulled the edges apart. Undressing him felt extraordinarily intimate, pleasurable. She had wanted to be here with him like this for days now. Finally, it was happening and his chest rose and fell with each slow, sensuous breath. She eased off his shirt, exposing his broad shoulders and muscular arms and the mat of dark brown hair spreading across his chest before arrowing down to the waistband of his trousers. She went up on tiptoe, kissing him yet again, the fabric of her dress brushing his hard muscles. She relieved him of his shoes, socks, undid his belt, released his pants. Leaving the boxer-briefs for last. When she had finished undraping him, she could only stare. He was more beautiful than she recalled, so aroused, so in need of her she felt her mouth go dry.

"My turn," he groaned, reaching around behind her and easing the zipper down, past her waist, to the small of her back.

He hooked his hands inside the sheath and eased it down, helped her step out of it. A rush of desire sweeping through her, clad only in a pale blue lace demibra, matching panties and thigh-high stockings, she faced him. There was no need to say anything. He obviously liked what he saw as much as she did.

She was trembling as he removed the rest of her clothing. She marveled at how someone so big and strong and male could have such a tender touch. And then his lips were on her breasts, drawing deep. Everything else in their world fell away. It was just the two of them, just this, as her body thrilled and tingled with everything he offered, everything she yearned to have.

Caroline moaned, running her hands through his hair, bringing him closer still, wanting more. He replaced his lips with the pads of his thumbs. Straightened, took her mouth with his, and kissed her some more.

Together, they danced backward toward her bed. Arms wrapped around each other, they tumbled onto it. The next thing Caroline knew, she was lying on her back. Jack parted her knees and lay between the cradle of her thighs. She arched up off the bed as his lips drifted lower, suckling gently. Her thighs fell even farther apart as Jack touched and stroked. She was teetering on the edge...loving the way this felt...loving him...even as she quivered and nearly shot up off the bed with the sweet, hot ferocity of her response.

When she'd recovered, she turned to look at him, and saw the satisfaction in his eyes. He eased between her legs with a masculine resolve that had her surrendering to him all over again.

Jack had thought he was far too suspicious and jaded to ever enjoy falling for a woman again. He'd been wrong. The process of becoming Caroline's lover was far more enticing and absorbing than he had ever dreamed anything could be.

For one thing, even though she was sophisticated as hell outside the bedroom, she seemed like a complete innocent in the bedroom. To the point, making love felt new to him, too.

As their eyes locked and the air between them charged with escalating desire and excitement, Jack felt more open to love and passion than he had been in his entire life. Yearning swept through him as he pressed up against her, luxuriating in the heat of her soft, silky skin. And he knew he would never be satisfied with just another roll or two or three in the hay. Despite the disparity that remained between them, he wanted more from her.

Much more...

Sending him a provocative look, she smoothed her hands over the muscles of his thighs, up his spine, back down to the small of his back and the curve of his buttocks, before guiding him onto his back and moving her palms to the most sensitive part of him.

Aware of the need that seemed to grow in him, even as it was met, Jack closed his eyes, lost in the feel of her sensual exploration of his body, the way she was taking possession of him, as surely and completely as he planned to take possession of her. Kiss followed kiss. Caress followed caress as she created an urgent need only she could ease. Sensations ran riot. Needing to possess her the way he had never possessed any woman, Jack moved so she was beneath him yet again. He stretched out on top of her, length to length, pulling her knees to his waist. Gently, he moved up and in, pushing his erection into her trembling wetness, until they fit together as snugly as a lock and catch.

Caroline cried out and arched against him, tempting him to move with tantalizing slowness…filling and retreating…seducing and taking…going ever deeper, ever slower…finding meaning…encouraging her to give back, even as she, too, demanded more. Until at last everything merged. Passion, tenderness, need and surrender. And the two of them held tight to each other as they soared, found release, and continued to hold on to everything they wanted, everything they had found.

Long minutes later, Jack still lay against the pillows, Caroline nestled against him. Her lower body rested between his legs. She had her head on his chest, one hand on his shoulder, the other on his waist. Their bodies were hot, and damp, and sated.

Jack had never been much for cuddling. But tonight he couldn't get enough of it. The feel of Caroline in his arms, all pliant, giving woman, satisfied him like nothing else he had ever experienced. He didn't know why or even how she had become such a big part of his life. He only knew that when she was with him, the sun shone a little brighter. And without her, the days seemed dull and long.

"So much for not being together again until after the wedding," Caroline murmured in drowsy defeat.

Jack frowned.

Back to reality once again.

And like it or not, that included the difficulties still facing them.

"If there is a wedding," Jack replied, determined not to let his growing feelings for Caroline and increasingly romantic view of the world make him think that everyone could be trusted the way he needed and wanted to trust them. Because it just wasn't so.

Caroline shot upright, clutching the sheet against her breasts. "Don't say that!"

Jack wasn't about to sugarcoat the situation, even to keep Caroline in that postlovemaking glow and ensure another chance to bring her to completion. "If the worst turns out to be true and Dutch does have an ulterior motive for marrying my mother—" he reminded gently.

"It won't." Temper gleamed in Caroline's blue eyes.

Jack wished he had Caroline's confidence. But the experience of being misled himself, even inadvertently, left him wary and on edge.

"But if it does—" Jack looked Caroline in the eye "—I will intervene."

Still holding his gaze, she dipped her head slightly in acknowledgment. Then said respectfully, "I know Dutch trying to raise a lot of money quickly looks bad, but there could be a very good reason he's so intent on liquefying all his assets."

"And if there is," Jack promised, "I'll find that, too."

"I'm still rooting for happily ever after," Caroline warned as they exchanged tentative smiles.

"Believe it or not," Jack said, kissing her gently and moving to make love to her again, "so am I." For his mother and Dutch. *And most especially, for the two of us....*

## *Chapter Eleven*

"Please go with us, Caroline!" Maddie begged late Monday afternoon, just minutes after getting home from school. She jerked the pastel cotton bucket hat off her head and waved it around like a coastguard signalman hoisting a flag. "I can't go on a walk with Bounder without a grown-up with us, and Daddy won't be home for a very long time!"

"Translated, that is thirty minutes," Patrice put in.

"See?" Maddie threw up her hands in dismay. "That's *forever!* And Bounder hasn't had a walk in the longest time ever. And now the vet says she's all healed and she can go, only Daddy's not here!"

"I need more time to study the portfolios of the photographers before I make a decision," Patrice said.

And they really needed her to make a decision. Caroline patted Maddie on the shoulder. "Then I'll go with you. But I have to warn you, I don't know much about walking a dog." Thus far, her interactions with pets had involved petting and cuddling them.

"Not to worry," Patrice interjected with an encouraging smile. "Bounder's well trained. She practically walks herself."

Exactly the kind of dog Caroline needed. "Well, then, we're off," she announced.

Maddie snapped on Bounder's leash and grabbed hold

of the long leather lead. For safety's sake, she handed the loop handle at the end to Caroline. Together, the two of them were out the door, dog in tow. The fact they were both holding on to the leash had them walking very close together. Looking down at Maddie, Caroline thought, this was what it would be like to have a daughter. To come home and spend time together at the end of every school day....

"Are you excited about the wedding?" Maddie asked as Bounder picked up the pace and pranced energetically down the walk, her fluffy golden tail wagging. "'Cause I am!"

Caroline struggled to keep pace. The strappy spring sandals she was wearing today were not meant for athletic activity. "Actually, I am really looking forward to it, too." This wedding was shaping up to be the most talked about ceremony in May. The thought made her smile.

Maddie skipped down the sidewalk. Her faster, energetic pace encouraged her dog to move more quickly, too. She pushed the brim of her hat out of her eyes. "Were you ever a flower girl?"

Briefly, Caroline lost her hold on the leash, then caught it again, and held tight. Thinking how cute Maddie looked in her denim shorts and Girls Rock! T-shirt, Caroline said, "No. I wasn't, sad to say."

Maddie came to a dead stop at the corner, clearly wondering which way. She rubbed the toe of her sneaker across the sidewalk curb. "That is sad!"

Caroline touched the little girl's shoulder and wordlessly pointed in the direction that would keep them from having to cross the street. "But I did a lot of other fun things when I was a kid."

Without warning, Bounder ground to a halt, causing the

two of them to nearly stumble over seventy-five pounds of dog.

Puzzled, Caroline looked down.

Bounder stood stock-still, ears back, head up, her whole body on alert. The golden retriever looked left, then front and center, then right.

Caroline's gaze focused on the quarry.

And suddenly, Caroline knew what the hubbub was all about. What was it that Jack had said about Bounder and trouble…?

"Maddie! Let go of the leash!" Caroline shouted implacably, still hanging on tight.

Fortunately, the startled Maddie did as Caroline commanded.

And it was a good thing, because Bounder took off like a shot after the offending bunny rabbit, who'd been hiding in the neighbor's flower bed. The bunny, no fool, took off, too, hopping like mad out of the blossoms, across the yard, past the sidewalk and into the street.

Caroline was dimly aware of an SUV coming toward them. "Stay where you are, Maddie!" she yelled, pushing the little girl back, far out of harm's way, at the same time she fought to gain control of the dog on the leash. A feat which proved impossible as the dog continued to give chase and sprinted out into the street. Caroline yelled, "Stop, Bounder!" To no avail. She was tugged along with the pet. As soon as Caroline cleared the curb, she yanked hard, bringing Bounder to a halt while the sound of squealing brakes rang in her ears.

They missed colliding with the vehicle, but there was nothing Caroline could do about the force of the backward motion. She lost her balance, so did Bounder. Both of them went down in a heap. It took only seconds to see that the dog's once injured paw was okay. Caroline's palms and both of her knees were bleeding.

Hands and legs stinging, Caroline stood on shaky legs, being careful to keep a tight hold on the leash.

Bounder stood, tail wagging, looking none the worse for wear, and still looking in the direction of the long-gone rabbit.

"Are you okay?" Maddie asked from the curb.

"That," a familiar voice said, as Jack stepped out from behind the wheel of the SUV, "is what I'd like to know."

"GRAM! CAROLINE'S A HERO!" Maddie shouted as the four of them came in the front door.

Patrice looked up from the sample wedding album photos.

Caroline knew she was a mess. She held up a gritty, still-burning palm. "I'm fine. Really." Although she felt like she was going to burst into tears at any moment, she wouldn't actually do it.

"What happened?" Patrice asked, horrified.

"Bounder saw a rabbit," Maddie supplied.

Patrice cringed, able to envision the ensuing commotion and fall to the ground. "I'll get the Band-Aids and disinfectant. Jack, show Caroline to the master bath to get washed up. She can sit on the edge of the tub while she cleans off those knees."

Caroline would have liked to protest. But since the scrapes had road dirt in them, she knew she'd better do as advised to prevent infection.

"Can I go?" Maddie asked.

"No, dear. Caroline needs her privacy. But you can help me in the kitchen…." Patrice laced her arm around her granddaughter's shoulders and guided her toward the rear of the house.

Caroline slipped off her sandals and followed Jack up the stairs. "I don't know what it is about you," she muttered as they passed through his ultramasculine bedroom and the bed where they had recklessly first made love, and walked into the adjacent bath, complete with glass-walled shower and garden-style soaking tub.

"I'm usually so well put together. But look at me." She gestured at her smudged black-and-white skirt and white sleeveless blouse that had been perfect for the warm spring day. "Once again, I'm a disheveled mess."

The corner of Jack's mouth crooked up. The heat in his gaze said he was recalling two other times when she'd been in a state of dishabille—for a completely different reason.

Eyes smoldering with sensual heat, he came nearer and wreathed a protective arm about her shoulders. "At least there's no blood on your clothes this time." Now that they were alone, he pressed a kiss on the top of her head, further marking her as his. "Just your knees." He kissed her again. Quickly, but more sensually this time.

Caroline drew back, aware her pulse had quickened as much as the rest of her. Aware the distraction had worked to dull the pain, she let herself relax. And looked deep into his eyes. "True," she murmured, glad she'd been there to take care of Maddie and Bounder, and glad Jack had been there to take care of her. "And I can also feel good about the fact that Bounder didn't reinjure her foot."

"That dog needs a refresher course for walking on a leash. I'm calling the trainer tonight." Jack gripped Caroline's hand. Gallantly, he helped her step over into the tub. Exuding tenderness, he provided extra support while she sat down. Then reached over and handed her the hand-spray nozzle, next to the tub spigot, and a bottle of liquid disinfectant hand soap. "I'll be glad to do that for you," he said, reaching over to first turn on and then adjust the temperature of the water coming out of the spout.

She looked at him wryly. He was taking chivalry to new heights. The only problem was, were Dutch, Maddie or Patrice to walk in and see, they'd know immediately that she and Jack were more than wedding planner and billable client.

That wouldn't look good to the adults.

And it wasn't something she wanted to be explaining, at this early date, to his daughter. Better to wait on that until they knew for sure that their relationship would continue.

"Thanks—" Caroline held up a staying hand "—but I think I can manage."

Jack got the message and, every bit the Texas gentleman, immediately backed off.

They hadn't seen each other since they had made love Saturday night. And since she still felt they really needed to hold off making their relationship a regular fling until after the wedding, no additional plans to get together intimately had been made.

That didn't mean she hadn't been thinking about him constantly. Wondering—or was it just plain hoping?—if this fling would turn into a whole heck of a lot more.

The look in his eyes said he had been thinking about her, too.

Caroline hitched up her skirt slightly, to make sure it didn't get wet, and then leaned over and lathered up her scraped hands.

The soap and water stung as it hit the open cuts. "It would have made more sense to clean my hands in the sink," she said. And still more sense just to go ahead and admit she was falling hard for Jack Gaines. That these emotions she was feeling weren't ever going to go away.

Instead of pretending they could stop what increasingly felt like a runaway train, anytime they wanted, and walk away unscathed.

"Hindsight," Jack teased, leaning one shoulder against the shower wall, "is always better." He widened his eyes with masculine appreciation as he facetiously took in the view.

Caroline's insides tingled. They were closer to making love again than she knew.

In fact, had they been anywhere else...

"Here you go!" Patrice said, bopping in with a box of Miss Kitty Band-Aids and painkilling antiseptic cream.

That quickly, Caroline was brought back to the present, and its restrictions on her behavior.

Caroline turned to Jack's mom. "Thank you."

Patrice caught Jack's happy aura. She beamed at the two of them, easily picking up on all that was left unspoken, then finally said to Jack, "I told you Caroline was someone special."

"A heroine indeed," Jack agreed. "Which brings us to the next topic of discussion," he said reluctantly. "After what happened just now...given that the wedding is outdoors, with all manner of wildlife possibly in the area... are we really sure we want Bounder to be part of the ceremony?"

Caroline knew what she thought.

"Bounder absolutely must take part," Patrice said.

"Mom," Jack chided.

"Maddie has spent so much time practicing her flower girl routine with Bounder already," Patrice pointed out. "You know she thinks of that dog as the sibling she lacks. She would be heartbroken if Bounder couldn't be there."

Jack looked to Caroline for support. "I have to agree with your mom," Caroline said. "It's Maddie's dream that she and her pet both be in the ceremony. I don't want to rob her of that."

"I don't, either," Jack said with a frown. "But given what happened just now…is a disruption to the wedding really a risk we want to take?"

"Yes," Caroline and Patrice said in unison.

"If it makes Maddie happy," Patrice said.

"And it will!" Caroline agreed.

"Now that we've got that settled…" Patrice swept back out, calling over her shoulder. "You-all take your time! Dutch is back. And he and I are starting dinner!"

As his mother retreated, silence returned. "I hope you and Mom are right about including Bounder in the wedding," Jack said.

"It'll be fine," Caroline reassured. "I've done half a dozen weddings on ranches in the last two years, and we've never had any unwelcome visitors yet. Probably because all the noise and confusion scares the critters away."

Jack relaxed. "I hadn't thought of it that way." He smiled. "In any case…" He stood, his tall body blocking the door to the master bath. Let his eyes track lazily over her, then drawled, "There is never a dull moment around here."

There was nothing dull about the way he was looking at her, or the wanted way it made her feel, Caroline thought.

Forcing herself to return to her task of cleaning up her wounds, Caroline winced as she washed the grit from her knees. "I remember now what I hated worst about being a kid," she moaned, wishing she could bypass this part of the process and go straight to the application of pain-numbing antiseptic cream. Catching Jack's tender expression, she joked, "Scraped elbows and hands and knees."

"Fall down a lot, did you?" Their brief disagreement over, Jack closed the distance between them and sat on the tub beside her. He took the sprayer and gently washed off one knee, and then the other. The sensation was exquisitely tender. She hadn't felt so cared for, or loved, since she could not remember when.

Caroline's breath caught. "All the time, when I was learning to ride my bike, and again when I learned to roller-skate." She paused and shook her head ruefully. "A lot of tumbles there. Also, when I was playing chase at recess and fell on the playground. What about you?" She turned toward him slightly, wondering, as she searched his face, if there was anything they could do together that wouldn't end up feeling intimate. "What kind of injuries did you incur?" she asked, curious about what he'd been like as a kid, before his dad got sick and he forgot how to dream.

Jack got a clean towel down from the shelf and blotted her knees and palms dry. "All of the above, plus bloody noses, a chipped tooth."

"No way!"

"Yep." He paused to point out the offending incisor.

Caroline studied his gleaming white teeth, noting nothing amiss. "It looks fine now."

Jack flashed a lopsided smile. "I had a dentist who could work wonders."

Caroline watched as Jack painstakingly applied antiseptic cream and two Band-Aids to each knee. "I wish I could have known you then."

"I wish I could have known you, too."

Their eyes locked. Jack leaned over, bracing a hand on the opposite side of her. Caroline saw the kiss coming. She welcomed it. The next thing she knew he had lifted her over onto his lap. Her arms were wreathed around his neck, and they were kissing like there was no tomorrow. Sweetly, deeply, tenderly. And that was when the bathroom door banged against the wall and an exuberant seven-year-old shouted at the top of her lungs, "Gram! Daddy and Caroline are *kissing!*" She danced in excitement and raced back out. "I think they're going to get married!"

"YOU CAN STOP blushing now," Jack teased as he walked Caroline out to her car several hours later.

Patrice and Dutch had finally decided on a wedding photographer. She had been booked for the event.

"You have to admit." Caroline ducked her head, remembering the excitement of both the other women in Jack's life. "It was awkward." Patrice had been pleased beyond measure at the developing romance.

Maddie had mistakenly concluded that their kiss meant Jack and Caroline would marry. And Maddie would then get the mommy she had recently been wishing for. Only Dutch wore a guarded expression, perhaps wondering if Caroline was making a mistake, getting involved with a man like Jack, who seemed to resist romance and the notion of happily ever after at every turn.

And that in turn had brought up all of Caroline's private misgivings. Could people change? Did she want to bank everything on Jack's inability to open his heart all the way and fall in love again? Or take the more optimistic route and hope that with time and patience he would find his inner romantic yet again? All she knew for certain was that she would never be really happy unless she was with a man who not only knew how important it was for her to hold a dream in her heart, but was also willing to share it and work for it, right alongside of her.

Jack touched her arm. "Are you speaking of before or after my mother gifted you with the perfume destined to make me fall in love with you?"

Not wanting to discuss the real reason behind her new

pensiveness, Caroline lifted the crystal bottle to her face and opened the cap. "It does smell heavenly." Like fragrant peaches, expensive champagne and a sun-warmed meadow. It brought to mind lazy, spring-fever days spent with a lover. And, despite her need to be cautious, that lover was Jack. Patrice had outdone herself with this fragrance. But Caroline suspected Jack's mother knew that.

Caroline juggled the gift basket of bath oil, scented soap, cologne, lotion and perfume—all laced with her new signature scent—and recapped the perfume.

Jack bent and inhaled the sensitive area just behind her ear. "Have to agree with you. That is really nice."

JACK HAD THOUGHT Caroline's devotion to making dreams come true without first stopping to make sure the dreams were worth pursuing, and his need to stop bad things from happening, had put them on a collision course. And while that still could be true in a worst-case scenario when it came to Dutch, Jack realized they also had a lot in common.

Like a fierce desire to shield those they cared about, a willingness to put themselves out there, the way she had by making sure his daughter stayed back and then jumped into the street with Bounder, instead of letting go of the leash and letting their dog face the danger alone.

Caroline had acted quickly and heroically in the exact same way he would have done in that situation, and that left him feeling closer to her than ever. "I really appreciate the way you went all out to protect Maddie and Bounder today."

Caroline rummaged through her purse for her car keys. "It was no problem."

Nor was their attraction to each other, Jack now knew. Even if they didn't see eye to eye on everything. They agreed on enough. "When can I see you again?" he persisted.

Caroline chuckled. "You're seeing me now."

He grinned at her teasing dodge. "Alone."

Caroline found her keys. Grew suddenly serious. "Are you sure it's wise? Given how much Maddie is beginning to want a mother. She was so over the moon just now when she saw us kissing. I don't want to hurt her."

"I don't want to hurt my daughter, either. And I still say, we'd be fools not to pursue this."

Jack returned Caroline's sober regard, waiting for what seemed an eternity. Finally, she gave in, as he hoped she would. She set the gift basket full of perfume in her car. "I guess it wouldn't hurt anything if we furthered our friendship."

Jack wanted a lot more than companionship from Caroline, but he would settle for what he could get. The full-on courting could come later....

"But all I've got available tomorrow is lunch."

Seeing her at noon sounded good. Hell, seeing her anytime, anywhere, sounded just fine. Jack made a mental note to adjust his own schedule. "Count me in." Not content to leave anything to chance, or give another guy a chance to move in on what he now considered his territory, he pressed, "What about Wednesday?"

Caroline bit her lower lip as she consulted the calendar on her BlackBerry, said finally, "I could do dinner."

Jack felt even happier. "I'll make reservations." Somewhere really nice.

She looked up with a sigh. "And nothing at all on Thursday."

Jack frowned in disappointment.

Caroline held up a hand before he could even attempt to persuade her otherwise. "Sorry, but Friday morning I head for the party ranch. I need to be there to receive the portable bathrooms and the two luxury motor homes the wedding party will get dressed in. The tents and the wedding arbor are going to have to be set up, extra flats of Texas wildflowers brought in and planted strategically around the wedding site, the chairs and portable stoves and refrigerators delivered. Bottom line, there is a lot to do. I'm going to need to get my beauty rest."

She had no idea how gorgeous she was, but he could not forget it. Still, he wanted her to feel good, and a little extra sleep would go a long way toward ensuring that.

Eager to be helpful, he said, "What time are you heading out Friday morning?"

"Six. I've got a lot to do."

There was no one Jack wanted to see more early in the morning. "How about I go with you?"

"I THINK IT'S A SPLENDID plan!" Patrice said when Jack told his mother of his decision to accompany Caroline to the wedding site later that same evening.

"My only quandary is whether to come back to Fort Worth Friday evening, or stay over and meet up with you and Dutch and Maddie and the rest of the guests on Saturday."

Patrice put down her newspaper. "You know what the romance gurus would say."

"Mom," Jack said sternly.

Patrice cast a fond glance at Dutch, who was outside on the patio talking on his cell phone, then turned back to Jack, merriment dancing in her gray eyes. "I'm just saying...."

Jack held up a staying palm. "I know what you and Maddie want." *And maybe I do, too.* "But there's only one Gaines family wedding happening this weekend," he finished firmly.

Patrice's smile was sly. "A mother can hope."

Jack saw his opening and took it with a gently voiced question. "Seriously, Mom." Jack leaned toward her, need-ing—wanting—to make certain. "Are you sure this is what you want to do?"

Disappointment reigned. "Jack!"

Unable to shake his feeling that something was amiss, Jack cast another look at Dutch, too. "If you have any doubts at all, we could reschedule for a later date."

Patrice rose. "I'm not waiting to marry Dutch. We're doing it this weekend, and we're doing it right." She stopped scowling long enough to touch Jack's shoulder with mater-nal affection. "Now stop worrying! If you don't stop you're going to get permanent frown lines on your forehead."

Like he cared about that. "That's what Botox is for."

"The day you are metrosexual enough to undertake a cosmetic procedure is the day I'll whistle Dixie through a pair of dentures!"

Jack laughed. "Okay, Mom. You've made your point."

He just hoped his mother was doing the right thing, and that nothing else potentially problematic turned up in his investigation of Dutch, because if it did, he was going to have to tell his mom a truth he was certain she would not want to hear.

The rest of the week passed swiftly. Jack and Caroline had a lunch and a dinner. They managed to talk on the phone late Thursday evening. On Friday, Jack arrived to pick her up at 6:00 a.m.

He had hoped the drive out to the party ranch would give them time to talk. Caroline spent the entire time on her cell phone, making sure that everyone was on schedule.

The only glitch was the scattered groupings of gray-blue

clouds dotting the horizon. Caroline got out of Jack's car. In deference to the hard physical labor she was going to be doing that day, she had on a waist-skimming white blouse, stack-heeled blue western boots and jeans.

Clipboard and BlackBerry in hand, she paused to look at the sky. "I checked the weather again this morning. The probability of a storm hitting the ranch is slight—less than ten percent."

Jack studied the storm clouds looming on the horizon. Another sign?

Caroline lit up at the half-dozen tractor trailers also headed their way. "Looks like we're right on schedule," she said, pleased.

By late morning, the white tents and the lights for the event had all been erected, the dance floor and bandstand set up, the outdoor kitchen hooked up and arranged. As those trucks and their workers left, several other tractor trailers, carrying the portable bathrooms, drove in. Those were followed by trucks delivering white folding chairs and the wedding arbor. The flowers weren't going to be set out until the next morning.

"Looking good," Jack told Caroline as Cinco de Mayo ribbons and streamers were set out along the drive from the highway onto the ranch, furthering the festive air.

"Except for one thing," Caroline grumbled as two luxury motor homes rumbled onto the property. She looked at the new bank of dark clouds looming on the horizon. "Yet another threat of rain."

Jack waved off her concern as his cell phone began to ring. "Bad weather's been passing us by all day."

Leaving Caroline to tell the delivery people where to set the motor homes that would serve as dressing and waiting rooms for the wedding party, Jack walked off to take the call.

Laura Tillman's voice sounded in Jack's ear. "I've got some news for you. And you're not going to like it...."

Jack listened to what the P.I. had to say with a sinking feeling in his gut. "Give me a call as soon as you know more," he instructed. She promised to do so and the conversation ended.

Jack managed to stay away from Caroline until the motor home deliverymen had left. The minute she came toward him, she knew something had changed. And not for the better. "What's going on?" she asked.

Jack looked at the racks of tarp-covered white folding chairs that wouldn't be set out until morning. Then at the ever-darkening blue-gray sky. Should he tell Caroline what they knew thus far? Or just wait until Laura had something more detailed?

"I can tell by the look on your face that something is up," Caroline insisted. She grasped his arm. "Don't even try and pretend otherwise. So you may as well just go ahead and tell me, because I'm not going to rest until I find out what's got you looking so concerned."

# Chapter Twelve

For a moment, Caroline thought Jack wasn't going to tell her anything. Then he scowled and reported reluctantly, "Laura's company set up surveillance."

Caroline's heartbeat kicked up a notch as she noted the air around them was getting uncomfortably warm and humid again. "And?" she prodded, hoping for the best while dreading the worst.

The lines on either side of Jack's handsome mouth deepened. "A pretty forty-something blonde has been seen coming in and out of Dutch's apartment when he's there. Apparently, they were together twice this week, both times for over four hours!"

Okay, Caroline thought. That didn't sound good. But it wasn't necessarily the disaster Jack was making it out to be, either. "Who is she?" Caroline asked calmly.

Jack clamped a hand over the tense muscles in his neck, then began to pace the lawn where the wedding would take place late the following afternoon. "Well, that's the problem," Jack said, grimacing, taking another look at the looming gray clouds. "We don't know yet."

Needing to get away from the increasing ferocity of the gusting wind blowing across the plain, Caroline stepped inside the tent where tables and chairs for the reception had already been set up. She walked over to a set of plastic-covered bins containing the elegant place cards and printed menus. She double-checked to make sure all was in order, and checked that off her list. "So this mystery woman could be anyone."

Jack followed her, hands shoved into the pockets of his jeans. "Like a mistress."

Caroline had hoped her influence would have Jack taking a more charitable view of his mother's fiancé. Obviously not. Yet, anyway. She still had hopes she could reform him. Caroline moved to the seating chart that would guide the waitstaff the next day. All was in order there, too.

"Or a professional colleague." Caroline continued theorizing optimistically. "It is traditional for the bride and groom to give each other gifts. The mystery woman could be working on a surprise for your mother on her wedding day. In fact, for all you know, she could be an artist, consigned to make a special piece of jewelry, or a travel agent finalizing the details of a luxurious Australian honeymoon. Dutch is in charge of that, you know, and he hasn't told your mother where they are going. Or even exactly when." But both the bride and groom were eagerly looking forward to it.

Jack perched on the edge of one of the circular tables, arms folded in front of him. Clearly, Caroline noted, he was back to thinking the worst about Dutch.

"I know you're trying to help, but you're reaching," Jack told Caroline grimly.

Caroline put down her clipboard and pen. "And, as always, you're suspecting the worst, instead of hoping for the best."

Jack threw up his hands in disgust. "Look, I want this to be innocent as much as you do."

"But you can't trust the mystery woman and her involvement in the situation any more than you can trust Dutch."

Jack reached out and pulled Caroline close, situating her between his spread legs. "You know the old saying," he murmured as her bottom settled comfortably on the inside of his muscular thigh. "If it looks bad, and it smells bad, it probably is bad."

Relishing the physical closeness of his body, Caroline splayed her hands across the warm, hard muscles of his chest. She looked into his eyes. "There's also an old saying that warns not to judge a book by its cover, especially if there could be a logical explanation for all of this."

"I might believe that," Jack said, "if all Dutch had done was try and liquidate his assets quickly or rent an apartment for himself that he's never mentioned having, or met with a pretty blonde twenty years my mother's junior a couple of times. But add all three things together...?"

Dutch had never seemed like a womanizer to Caroline. Diligently, she tried another tact. "For all we know these three things are connected and this young woman is a real estate broker who is working with Dutch on selling all his beachfront properties ASAP."

Another gust of wind lifted the flap on the tent, and shook the fabric overhead.

Caroline slid off Jack's lap. She spoke over her shoulder as she headed toward the exit for a look-see. "Listing a property involves a lot of paperwork and can be very time-consuming."

Jack ambled after her. "Then why not tell us that he's going off to meet a business contact? Or have that person come to the house to work with him while Maddie is in school?"

Caroline shrugged as fat drops of rain hit the ground in staccato bursts. "Maybe Dutch wanted privacy to conduct his financial transactions." She swiveled around to face Jack as the sky grew ever darker and another burst of wind shook the tent. "Maybe he's embarrassed he hasn't been able to quickly divest himself of his business holdings on his own. Maybe your mother knows about this woman and the meetings and just hasn't said anything to you because she doesn't think it's any of your business." Caroline tilted her chin. "The bottom line is we already know Dutch is in a hurry to get out of the property rental and management business altogether so he can officially retire, just as your mother has, and not have to worry about it. So it figures— even if he's not talking about it to us—that Dutch would be putting a lot of energy into making it happen, even from afar."

Jack considered her point, looking as if he wanted to believe as Caroline did that a happily ever after was still possible for his long-widowed mother. "Then why not rent virtual office space—which is available on a month-to-month basis?" Jack countered, stubborn as ever. He searched Caroline's eyes. "Why an apartment?"

There were many possible reasons, Caroline thought. She shrugged as a crack of lightning flared in the distance and caught their eyes. She turned to see what looked like a heavy rainstorm moving quickly across the plain. Gosh, those clouds were getting dark!

Knowing a tent was not a good place to weather the approaching electrical storm, Caroline grabbed Jack's hand. As thunder rumbled in the distance and rain dampened their clothes, they dashed toward the safety of the luxury motor homes. "He's older. He's used to living alone. It's possible he wanted a more comfortable place to work as well as a place where he could escape if life at your house got too hectic. And you have to admit, it can be a little lively there, with Maddie and Bounder, and your mom and you…especially if…" Caroline made a little joke as she opened the door and vaulted up the steps and inside "…Bounder catches sight of a rabbit."

Pausing to acknowledge the memory of that unexpected calamity and others that were doubtless still to come, Jack followed her into the motor home. "Dutch has never behaved like bedlam bothered him. He's acted as if he loved the commotion of our household, the same as you do!"

So Jack had noticed how easily she had blended into his family, Caroline thought happily as she went into the bath and came out with two hand towels. She handed one to Jack and used the other to blot the raindrops from her face. She wanted the joy she felt at being with Jack to spread to all aspects of their lives.

As they stood there, staring at each other, Caroline abruptly became aware of two things.

One, it sounded like the rain had completely stopped.

And two, it had gotten incredibly dark all of a sudden.

Almost as black as night.

And then they heard it, a roar like a train.

They swore simultaneously. Jack grabbed her hand and pulled her out of the motor home. A half a mile from them, a funnel cloud was hovering just above the fence line. And it was headed straight for the wedding site!

They swore again and took off for the ditch that ran along either side of the drive. Jack pushed her into it, and dove down on top of her, draping her with his length, holding her tight.

Caroline shut her eyes, praying, and the world slowed.

The noise grew deafening.

The ground trembled.

She and Jack were lifted slightly, set back down.

And then all grew silent once again.

WAS IT OVER? Jack wondered. It sure as heck seemed like it was. But then, right now he wasn't sure of anything, except that beneath him Caroline was okay, and his heart was pounding so hard it felt like it would leap out of his chest. Taking his cue from the absence of wind and sound, Jack eased his weight off of Caroline slightly and lifted his head.

It was over, all right. And it was pouring down rain.

Jack pushed himself out of the ditch. Caroline followed suit, and with his help, struggled to her feet, too. She wrapped her arms around him. "Jack," she said fiercely.

He hugged her back, just as hard, relishing the feel of her body, the knowledge she was safe from harm. Over the top of her head, Jack scanned their surroundings, taking note of what had happened, trying to make sense of everything he saw. It was easy to see where the tornado had touched down. It had kicked up sod and fence in a jagged line along the perimeter of the party ranch, but miraculously had changed course at the last minute and done only minor damage to the party tents. One rack of chairs had been upended and scattered across the lawn where the guests would be seated. The wedding arbor had been yanked out of the ground by the force of the wind and torn to bits as well, Jack noted grimly, thinking of the ceremony that was to take place in that exact spot the following day. But the motor homes, the portable restrooms, even the outdoor kitchen that had been set up for the caterers, all looked mostly untouched.

Caroline, however, still looked pretty badly shaken up, and her face and clothing were smudged with rain and dirt.

Jack wrapped his arm around her. He pressed a kiss on the top of her head. "Let's get you inside."

Once in the safety of the motor home, Caroline excused

herself and slipped into the bathroom. He grinned as he heard her exclamation of dismay. Obviously, she'd caught sight of herself in the mirror.

Then frowned as he tried to turn on the lights, and got no response.

The tap turned on, then ten seconds later abruptly stopped.

Caroline came back out of the bathroom.

"There's no water and the lights aren't working."

"The connections to the ranch power and water supply could have been knocked loose in the storm," Jack theorized. *Or it could be a larger problem....* "Let's try the guest restrooms."

They left the motor home and went to the luxury bathrooms trucked in for the occasion. Same result. They stepped back outside. The rain was still coming down, drenching everything in sight. Coming toward them was a familiar pickup truck. It stopped just short of them and the owner of Ted's Party Ranch stepped out. Unlike them, he was clad in a yellow rain slicker, and looked none the worse for the calamity.

"Y'all okay?" the cowboy asked.

They nodded. "Except for the loss of power," Jack said.

"Yeah, well." Ted stroked his handlebar mustache and scraggly goatee. "That's what I came to talk to you about. The power's out. The storm took out a couple of towers between here and the station."

"That sounds bad," Caroline said.

Ted nodded. "It is. I just talked to the electric company. They're saying it will be early next week before they can get the towers replaced and the lines back up."

"Which is why the water's out, too," Jack surmised.

Caroline looked at him, perplexed.

"We're on well water," Ted explained. "Without electricity, the pumps won't work. So, there's no water. Without water, there's no way to provide for the facilities, not for three hundred people."

Caroline scowled at Jack, her dreams for the perfectly planned and executed wedding fading fast. "If you say this is another sign…" Caroline warned Jack stonily.

She looked like she didn't know whether to kick something in frustration or burst into tears, Jack noted sympathetically. And might just do both. There was only one way, Jack knew, to save the day. "Let me call the guys," he said, ready, willing and able to be her hero once again. "And we'll see what we can do."

HALF AN HOUR LATER, help was on its way, and Dutch and Patrice were on the phone with Jack. "Thank heaven we found you!" Patrice said the moment Jack said hello via the speakerphone on his cell. "Dutch and I just saw the news report of the tornado that touched down in your area! Are you and Caroline all right?"

How long, Caroline wondered, since she'd had "family" worrying about her, checking up on her, making sure she was okay? How long since she'd felt part of something larger than just herself?

Jack wrapped his arm around Caroline's shoulders and brought her in close so she could participate in the conversation, too. "We're fine, Mom."

"We're very glad to hear that," Dutch said in obvious relief.

"Massive power outages in the area were also reported," Patrice continued.

Jack hadn't wanted his mother to know this, for fear she'd worry. "That's true, Mom, but we're working to fix it as we speak," Jack reassured over the sound of the rain still hammering the motor home roof above.

"I can't believe this is happening," Patrice choked out, distraught. "We're supposed to get married tomorrow, Dutch!"

"Now, honey," Dutch soothed in a tender tone that had Caroline envisioning the older gentleman wrapping his arms around Patrice, comforting his bride-to-be in the same way Jack was now comforting her. "I told you, there's no use fighting Mother Nature. If need be, we'll just re-schedule. Or move the wedding indoors. Or even go to a justice of the peace, whatever you want." To his credit, Dutch seemed amenable with whatever happened.

"Fortunately," Caroline interrupted firmly, resuming her role of wedding planner in command, "neither option is going to be necessary." That was, if Jack and his friends managed to accomplish all the things they had promised in the short amount of time they had left. "Although it's pouring right now, the rain here is supposed to end by early evening."

"You see, honey?" Dutch told Patrice gently. "Everything is going to be all right."

A tremulous sigh. Then a pause. "I know, dear. We just need to have faith."

Caroline's certainty that this couple was meant to be together increased. Jack looked touched by the affection of their exchange, too. There was no doubt about it, Dutch was good for his mother.

"It's going to be fine, sweetheart," Dutch comforted Patrice gently. "I promise."

In the background, a door slammed. There were the sounds of running footsteps and a loud woof, then Maddie coming in, shouting, "Gram! Is that Daddy on the phone?

'Cause you're not going to believe it! Because Bounder saw another rabbit! Can I talk…?"

And that was the end of all serious conversation.

"TELL ME AGAIN. Why are we doing this?" Grady asked several hours later.

"Seems to me," Travis said, hooking up the strategically placed portable generators Jack had commissioned and brought out to the site by his four best friends, "this is the perfect excuse to slow things down regarding your mom and Dutch. If that is indeed what you want."

The irony of his actions were not lost on Jack. Five hours ago, he'd been ready to go to his mother, tell her what he knew thus far, and let the chips fall where they may. Then the storm had come along. Once again, the calm of his life had been disrupted by the unexpected.

He thought about the defeated look on Caroline's face when she realized the wedding might have to be canceled or delayed, and the fact that he had never before seen her look defeated, or even imagined he could.

"Caroline has a lot riding on this," Jack allowed finally.

The guys exchanged looks.

"So do you," Nate advised, with the reserve of the only bachelor in the group. "And so does your mom."

Jack thought about when his mother had heard there had been a tornado in the area and she and her fiancé had called to confirm he and Caroline were okay.

There'd been something in his mother's and Dutch's voices when they called that Jack hadn't heard since his dad was alive. Finally, he saw what Caroline had apparently intuited for a while now, that Dutch and his mom had that something special.

"I'm beginning to think—" or was it just wish, Jack

wondered silently, because he cared so much about Caroline and wanted her to succeed in her ventures as much as he wanted to shelter the rest of his family from harm? "—that I might be overreacting to the swiftness of the nuptials."

Silence fell among the guys. "If there's one thing I've learned," Dan shared, referencing the huge mistake he'd made with Emily, when he'd tried to save the day in a similar overbearing way, "is that while women like us to offer plenty of emotional support during the process, they want to make their own decisions and solve their own problems."

But how could his mother do that, Jack wondered, without all the information? Were feminine intuition and pure emotion enough? Or were cold, hard facts required, too?

"I NEVER THOUGHT we'd get this done," Caroline told Jack shortly after 2:00 a.m., when they met up in the motor home to compare notes, after everyone but the two of them had left the party ranch. She gulped springwater from a bottle. "You really came through for me, figuring out a way to provide enough power and get everything hooked up, then calling in all your friends to make it happen."

Jack wished he could be happier about that. The truth was, he still felt a little conflicted.

If time was on his side, Jack mused, Laura Tillman would come through with the final details of her investigation tomorrow as promised, and he would soon learn that the blonde visiting Dutch at his apartment had good reason for being there. Then he could finally relax and give Dutch and his mother the wholehearted blessing they sought. But right now he only had one goal in mind. Offering Caroline the emotional support she needed.

He waited until she had drained the bottle and put it

aside, then stepped behind her and massaged the stiffness from her shoulders. "What time are the writer and photographer from *Fort Worth* magazine showing up tomorrow?"

Caroline closed her eyes and let her head fall back in surrender. Her silky copper curls brushed the backs of his hands. "They are supposed to be here at nine." Her body warmed beneath his kneading fingers, even as she stifled a yawn. "They want to capture all the behind-the-scenes pre-wedding stuff as well as the actual ceremony and reception."

Jack smiled as she sank deeper into his touch and moved her head from side to side. "What's the weather?"

Caroline stood upright. She widened her eyes and reported with comic gravity, "Well, for starters, there is zero chance of rain and/or tornadoes tomorrow!" She caught his glance then smiled, content. "The temperature is going to be eighty, with very low humidity and a light breeze."

Or in other words, Jack thought, the perfect spring day in Texas. "So it should be very comfortable," he surmised.

Caroline nodded. "I think so."

"How about everything else?" Jack asked.

"Good. The florist is bringing a new arbor first thing tomorrow. The catering service has arranged to replace the portable stove that was blown over. I'm confident it's all going to go off without a hitch, despite the storm." She paused. "Seriously, Jack, I do owe you for all you did for me tonight."

Gratitude was not what he wanted. But figuring any serious discussions on the subject could and should wait, he teased back, "Remind me to collect on the debt."

Caroline's laughter turned into something sweeter, more erotic. She glided into his arms, looked as if she needed an outlet for all the excess adrenaline as much as he did.

She wreathed her arms around his neck and tilted her face up to his. "Why put off until tomorrow what you can do today?"

"Why, indeed," Jack agreed.

He bent his head and took her lips, let himself revel in the taste and feel of her, so soft and womanly.

Caroline sighed in pleasure. "I knew we'd end up like this tonight."

She rose on tiptoe, pressing the warmth of her body against his. The small sign of surrender was all it took. His gentlemanly restraint fled. He danced her backward, toward the wall, and held her captive there. Their kiss intensified, going on and on. She opened her mouth to the plundering pressure of his. Let her body yield, oh so sweetly.

Jack wanted to tell Caroline that being with her like this was changing his life. Making him want it all again. Giving the courage to take a risk and open up his heart the way it hadn't been in years. Not sure she would believe him if he did—not sure he believed it quite yet—he tried to show her how he felt instead.

Need radiating through him, he tangled his fingers in her hair and kissed her with absolutely nothing held back. Kissed her until she was moaning low in her throat and responding just as ardently, as thoroughly and completely as if she might be falling in love with him, too.

Determined to take his time and make it last, he unbuttoned her blouse and opened up her bra. She gasped as he covered her breasts with his hands, and felt the nipples bud against his palms, then shuddered again as his mouth followed the path his hands had blazed. Jack dropped to his knees, found the snap and zipper on her mud-splattered jeans.

Inside, the skin was just as hot and silky soft as the rest

of her. She groaned as he pushed the cloth past her knees
and found her again, tracing the sweet perfection of her.
Holding her captive, he moved a hand between their bodies,
and touched and rubbed and stroked. Kissed and adored,
until her body was arching up instinctively. Finding her
ready for love, he rose again, stepped out of his pants,
finished divesting her of hers, and slid his hands beneath
her hips.

She wanted him and he wanted her, too. So badly. Hands
under her hips, he lifted her. She wrapped her legs around
his waist, showing him how well they fit, enveloping him
in a way that felt so right, engendering a need within both
of them that felt so incredible and real it would not be
denied.

Caroline had known making love would deepen their
relationship. She hadn't expected that the raw power and
the beauty of the physical act would cause her to open up
her heart and her soul in a way it had never been before.
But that was exactly what was happening.

She was in love with Jack. Head over heels in love with
him. So it was no surprise how much this meant to her. No
stopping the abandon that overtook her whenever he held
her in his arms. No fighting the free-falling ecstasy that
filled her heart and warmed her soul as the fire between
them burned hotter and hotter.

In three short weeks, Jack had become everything to her.
The mate she had always wanted, the friend and companion she needed, the protector and lover she had to have.

There was no more denying it, Caroline thought, as
together they surged toward new heights. The two of them
belonged together, not just for now, but for all time.

## Chapter Thirteen

"This is shaping up to be one fantastic wedding," Jericho remarked as he added the finishing touches to the ten-tiered *dulce de leche* wedding cake and the chocolate Kahlua groom's cake.

"I have to admit," Caroline said, "it's turning out better than I could have dreamed." The photographer and reporter from *Fort Worth* magazine had arrived early and were busy chronicling every aspect of the wedding, down to the tiniest detail.

Jack had spent the morning alternately riding herd on Maddie and Bounder, which was no easy feat. Both were incredibly excited about their upcoming trip down the aisle.

Dutch and Patrice were behind closed doors, in their respective motor homes, getting ready for the ceremony with the help of their eight attendants.

Meanwhile, a solid line of cars was turning onto the festively decorated lane leading to the wedding site.

Some two hundred and fifty guests had already arrived and were seated in the white folding chairs on the brilliant green lawn. Colorful Cinco de Mayo banners waved in the wind, and whiskey barrels overflowing with Texas wildflowers added additional color along the aisles and in every nook and cranny. A mariachi band was playing traditional love songs of both Texas and Mexico, while a bevy of traditional dancers was dressed and ready to perform at the reception.

"And," Jericho continued, "it looks like the son of the bride has a thing for you."

Caroline flushed. Although she and Jack had been up most of the night making love, they had been so focused on their dual responsibilities, the two had barely spent any time together since. She watched Jericho pipe on a delicate wildflower border of Texas bluebonnets across the bottom of the cake. "Where did you get that idea?"

Jericho's dreadlocks bounced against his shoulder as he worked. "Honey, I know two people in love when I see them."

Caroline knew she was in love. Jack, on the other hand, had never put his feelings into words.

"His daughter, Maddie, and that pup of hers seem to adore you, too."

That was true, Caroline thought.

"Although," Jericho declared, straightening, and changing out pastry tubes, "I think people who put dogs in ceremonies are crazy."

"Bounder is very well behaved." Except, Caroline added mentally, remembering her still-skinned knees, when she sees a rabbit. Fortunately, Caroline hadn't seen any hopping around the ranch. Maybe the storm had scared them all away? Or simply too much commotion?

"Famous last words," Jericho intoned, going back to work to fix a slightly lopsided green leaf made out of frosting.

Caroline felt a little jump of nerves. Her career was riding on a successful outcome today. A positive review would make her the up-and-coming wedding planner to hire. Whereas a negative one...

"In fact," Jericho went on, moving to the groom's cake to make sure all was in order there, too, "judging by the way Dutch and Patrice are interacting with you, you seem to have hit it off with Jack's entire family."

"They're easy people to get to know," Caroline replied, watching as her assistant, Sela Ramirez, rode herd on the catering staff setting up for the reception in an adjacent tent.

"Yeah, well, all I can say, darlin', is that you make it look easy."

Falling in love with Jack, becoming part of his world, felt easy, Caroline thought. In one fell swoop she would have the husband of her dreams, a delightful daughter, an adorable dog and Patrice and Dutch, too. The only problem was, making all her best dreams come true had never been an easy task. All her best dreams had required hard work, dedication and time. A lot more time than she had spent with Jack thus far.

"Uh-oh," Jericho murmured, staring at the statuesque redhead gunning straight for Jack. "Who's that?"

Laura Tillman, Caroline thought with an inward groan of dismay, the private investigator checking out Dutch.

JACK ASKED GRADY TO KEEP an eye on his daughter and Bounder, who were both still giddy with excitement over their impending flower girl and flower dog trek down the aisle. He caught Caroline's eye, indicating he'd like her to join them, then escorted Laura Tillman into the dining tent. The linen-covered tables were set with heavy antique silver, fiesta-colored china, handmade white candles and copper urns of Texas wildflowers. Behind the table, where the bride and groom would sit with their attendants, was a spectacular white wedding piñata, shaped like a leaping deer, hanging from a large wooden post. Twin white satin blindfolds and sticks were placed nearby. It was a clever way to include the traditional breaking of the party piñata, and lent a memorably eclectic touch to a wedding that was both breathtakingly beautiful and rustically Texan.

"Sorry it took me so long to get here," Laura said as Caroline walked up to join them. Laura handed over the file. "But I figured you would want to have the information in hand, if you decided to speak to your mother."

Jack's gut twisted. He exchanged apprehensive looks with Caroline, then turned back to Laura. "I take it you know the identity of the mystery woman."

The P.I. nodded. "Her name is Maryellen Innes. She's forty-two years old, has three kids, and is by all accounts very happily married."

Beside Jack, Caroline relaxed.

Laura continued. "She's also a registered nurse, who specializes in home care. Specifically, dialysis."

This, Jack hadn't expected, nor had Caroline. Dutch looked so healthy. But then, Jack thought, so had his dad when he was diagnosed with ALS. Jack swallowed around the lump of emotion in his throat. "You're saying...?"

The P.I. grimaced in frustration. "Medical records are private, protected by law. So it's impossible to know for sure what was going on between the two. What I can tell you, after further investigation, is that Maryellen Innes has been chatting with Dutch regularly on the phone, and visiting Dutch roughly three times a week at the apartment for four hours at a time, ever since he arrived in Fort Worth several months ago. At-home dialysis takes approximately four hours and is generally scheduled at that interval."

"Which means that Dutch could be in kidney failure," Jack concluded soberly as Caroline reached over and gently touched his arm.

"It's entirely possible," the investigator agreed.

They all paused to consider that. "If so," Caroline reflected eventually, compassionate as ever, "it would certainly explain a lot. Dutch's trip to Houston, his time with the nephrologist. Possibly even the decision to sell all his properties in a hurry, if he needed money for a transplant."

"The only way to find that out is to confront Dutch and ask him what his situation is," the P.I. said. "And again, I'm sorry I couldn't get this information to you sooner."

"I appreciate the hard work," Jack said.

The P.I. nodded and exited the tent.

Caroline and Jack squared off. "I can see you're worried," she said softly, "but I'm sure everything is going to be all right."

Jack couldn't believe she was still cheerleading for Dutch. "It will be, once I talk to my mother and let her know what the situation is," Jack countered grimly.

Caroline caught his arm, tugged him back. "It's one thing for you to do a little sleuthing behind the scenes for your own peace of mind," she warned, upset. "I get that you needed to know Dutch wasn't a con artist out to steal your mother's money. It's something else entirely for you to try to interfere with or derail your mother's plans for her life. I know how close those two are. I've seen them fall more and more in love with each other with every day that has passed. If Dutch is sick, your mother must know."

"And if she doesn't?" Jack demanded.

Caroline glanced at her watch. In the foreground, they could hear the musicians switch to a traditional wedding prelude program. "At least go to Dutch first, talk to him," she pleaded.

Jack exhaled. "And leave my mother out of the discussion? Isn't that what your ex-fiancé did? Go behind your back to try and assure a certain outcome?"

"That's the point, Jack," Caroline countered urgently. "You wouldn't be determining for your mother whether or not she marries Dutch. You would be sparing her the hurt and humiliation of a stalled or cancelled wedding. Because, believe me, having been there and seen that happen to even a small number of brides—it's nothing I would wish on anyone. Not if it can be at all avoided."

The last thing Jack wanted to do was publicly embarrass his mother in front of all her friends, never mind the press! Because Caroline was right about one thing—the cancellation of a wedding of two Texans as well-known as Dutch and his mother would be news. Speculation would abound. Jack couldn't stand to see his mother suffer any more than what she had already endured. Which was why...

As if reading his mind, Caroline caught Jack's hand and held on tight. "I understand how serious this situation is, Jack." Caroline looked deep into his eyes. "But don't you see that this is all the more reason to trust in Dutch and in your mother, to believe that your mother is old enough and wise enough to know what she is doing in marrying Dutch?"

"And if she isn't?" Jack asked wearily, wishing he had never been put in this situation. But he had been. And he knew what his dad would expect him to do.

Caroline, however, had other ideas. She squeezed his hand, hard. "I believe in this dream they have of spending the rest of their lives together," she said passionately.

Jack wished he could tell Caroline what she wanted, needed to hear from him. He couldn't. "I don't have the faith in their judgment that you do," he countered sadly. "Especially if you're right, and my mother knows what she is getting into. Because I remember all too vividly the pain of watching my father succumb to a devastating illness. I remember how grief-stricken and vulnerable my mother was at the end, how difficult it was for her to let go, never mind recover." The ache in his throat matched the unchecked grief deep inside him. "I never want to see her that sad and distraught again."

But for Caroline, Jack noted with growing disillusion-ment, the past—sad as it was—was over. Today was all about the future and the romance of their wedding, the illusion that the ideal happiness of this one exceptionally perfect day would last forever. Unfortunately, hiding from the truth, pretending it did not exist, would help no one. "And that means," Jack continued, "bad timing or not, I have to talk to my mother and Dutch together."

Caroline shook her head at him and stepped back, as if not knowing where to even to begin to argue with him. Scowling, she planted her hands on her hips and stared at him with a mixture of disappointment and disbelief. "You'd really go to them *now,* twenty minutes before they are to walk down the aisle, and try and ruin things!"

Why couldn't Caroline understand he had no choice in the matter? Determined to make her see, Jack weathered Caroline's incredulity with the same calm deliberation he did everything else. He angled a thumb at the center of his chest and stated flatly, "This is who I am." And he wouldn't apologize for it. "I'm the guy with no illusions. The guy who does the things that need to be done even if they are unpleasant."

"The guy," Caroline added to the list with an uncom-plimentary look of her own, "who has forgotten how to take the kind of risks that lead to love."

What the hell was she talking about! It was his concern for her and his family that had them in this mess! "And it's also why we can't be together," Caroline said.

Jack hardened his heart against further hurt and disap-pointment. Forced himself to be reasonable, even if it hurt.

"You can't mean that." What was going on with Dutch and his mom had nothing to do with them.

"Yes, Jack, I do," Caroline said quietly. She trod closer. But not close enough that he could touch her. Sadly, she continued. "I can't be with someone who has lost the ability to hold a dream in his heart, or honor someone else's." Unable to hide her resentment any longer, she leaned toward him. "Because if you could do that, Jack, you would understand why—if Dutch really is sick—that it is more important than ever for him and your mother to be together, and hold on to what time Dutch does have left with everything they've got."

Intellectually, Jack knew that. He had compassion for Dutch. And yet—he had a family to protect, too. To knowingly and willingly bring on that kind of heartache was something he just couldn't do. "I can't pretend to be some gullible kid, Caroline," Jack countered. "Not after the life I've lived. I can't pretend not to know the pain of living with life-threatening illness, of watching someone you love die, degree by degree."

"I'm not asking you to be naive," Caroline implored in a low, choked voice. "I'm asking you to understand how important it is to support the dreams of others, whether we agree with their goals or not. Because at the end of the day, Jack," she stressed emotionally, "our dreams are the only thing we have that can lead us to true happiness."

"I can't do that," Jack said, determined to deal with this situation calmly, even if she wouldn't. "Not when it comes to my mother and Dutch. Not knowing what I do now." He couldn't let his mother walk into a trap.

Caroline's jaw took on the stubborn tilt he knew so well. She threw up her hands and sent him a beleaguered smile that matched the turbulent emotion in her eyes. "Then you and I have nothing else to say."

He stared at her, incredulous she would let this break them up. "You're telling me it's over?" he ascertained in bitter disbelief.

"And then some." Caroline gave him one last heartbroken look and walked away.

He tipped aside the bottle to pour Patrice to the brim, after which he did the same for Dutch. He then lifted his own glass high.

And then said, "To the newlyweds and the man that made you both so lucky."

## Chapter Fourteen

Patrice and Dutch squared off with Jack in the luxury motor home that up to now had been serving as a dressing room for the bride. Now, it had been cleared of everyone except the three of them.

To Jack's consternation, Patrice refused to acknowledge the seriousness of the situation. She elbowed Dutch in the side, as if eliciting a laugh. "It's a good thing you and I aren't the superstitious type," she joked. "Otherwise, our wedding would be doomed."

Dutch bent down to kiss his bride lightly on the lips. "In my opinion, it can only be good luck for us to see each other before the ceremony."

Patrice turned to Dutch, wrapped her arms around his neck and brought his head down to hers. The two kissed with a lot more passion and verve than Jack had ever expected. In fact, had it not been his mother in the clinch, he would have said, "Get a room!"

Aware he really did not need to see this, he closed his eyes and ran a hand over his face. Cleared his throat. Loudly. Then heard the chuckling, the rustle of clothing as Dutch and Patrice moved apart.

Jack opened his eyes and studied his mother and the man who would soon be his stepfather, if all went their way. He wanted to think the two of them weren't head over heels in lust and in love. Three weeks ago, he was fairly certain that hadn't been the case. Now...all he knew for sure was that this kind of passion was hard to fake, and even harder to obtain. He could vouch for this because he'd discovered that kind of intense emotion with Caroline. Until today, anyway, when Caroline had resolutely given him the old heave-ho....

Dutch and Patrice looked at him. "We're waiting," his mother prodded impatiently.

Not sure where to begin, Jack simply handed over the P.I. report regarding the apartment and the visiting registered nurse who had been calling on Dutch three times a week.

Patrice scanned both documents, then sighed. Her expression unflappable, she sat down on the sofa against the window and patted the place beside her for Dutch. He sat down next to her, and still serious, took her hand in his. Patrice shook her head in dismay, even as she looked deeply into Dutch's eyes. "I told you Jack would find out your health is not as good as we'd like."

Jack paused, not sure what to think. "So you knew?" he asked, incredulous.

"That Dutch is on the kidney transplant waiting list?" Patrice scoffed and waved a hand. "Of course. Although if this new clinical trial accepts him as a patient, surgery may not be necessary after all. We're still waiting to hear from his Houston nephrologist on that. But either way, it doesn't matter. I told Dutch from the outset, I am in this for the long haul. Whether this new drug rejuvenates his failing kidneys, or he stays on at-home dialysis or opts for a transplant, Dutch is going to need someone by his side and I'm going to be there, Jack, whether you like it or not."

Jack studied them. He couldn't say he was totally surprised about his mother's generosity. She had always possessed an enormous heart. As well as a very good health insurance plan that—thanks to her lucrative deal with Couture Perfume—would continue for life, for herself and any dependents.

"Tell me this isn't about money and insurance," he insisted.

Patrice shrugged. "It certainly started out that way."

Once more, Jack found himself doing a double take.

Patrice leaned back against the cushioned seat and crossed her legs at the knee. "Of course, Dutch didn't want to get involved with me for that very reason, and I admit, I had a few reservations about becoming emotionally involved with anyone again myself."

"So we decided to become just friends instead," Dutch said. "And support each other that way."

"Which was great, because there was no pressure to move things along and we found we had a lot in common," Patrice enthused happily.

"The kind of simpatico that comes along all too infrequently in this life," Dutch said quietly.

"But then, several things happened," Patrice continued frankly. "Dutch's insurance plan was about to hit its benefit limit. He couldn't find another company that would underwrite the potentially enormous costs to contain or cure his illness. And he couldn't sell his properties on South Padre Island to secure his future and pay for the very latest treatments that way. So, we decided to marry. And before you say anything, Jack—" Patrice held up a warning hand "—this is a real marriage. To do otherwise, and collect money from a company, would be fraud. So Dutch and I knew from the outset that if we were going to do this, it had to be a true union. Which is why we wanted a big wedding with all the pomp and circumstance. Because we knew we needed to make it real for ourselves in every way."

"Only, a funny thing happened on the way to Ted's Party Ranch," Dutch teased.

"As we were going through the wedding preparations, we actually did fall in love," Patrice said softly.

"Very much in love," Dutch agreed, squeezing Patrice's hand.

"But not to worry. We are keeping our prenuptial agreements intact. My money remains mine. Dutch's remains his. And he won't even need to use my health insurance if Dutch is accepted into the clinical trial, because then all his expenses will be paid by the researchers."

Okay, from a business point of view, perhaps even a humane one, this all made a great deal of sense. That didn't mean Jack was completely okay with it. "I still worry about how hard this will be on you if all doesn't go as well as you and Dutch hope, with his quest for a return to good health," Jack said.

Patrice stood and came over to give Jack a hug. She drew back and counseled gently, "Honey, I appreciate the fact you're trying to protect me. But it just isn't possible. None of us know what tomorrow is going to bring. The only thing we can count on is the happiness we feel today."

ONE HUNDRED FEET AWAY, Sela Ramirez nodded at the luxury motor home, then asked Caroline, "What do you think is happening in there?"

"Exactly what you think is happening." Caroline was almost afraid to imagine the confrontation. She turned to face her sage assistant and predicted sadly, "Jack is revealing all and doing his level best to get his mother and Dutch to call off their wedding."

Sela did not share Caroline's heartbreak over the situation. "Jack may not have been duty bound to investigate Dutch—"

Caroline snorted. "You think?"

"But once he did, he had to tell his mother what he found out about her fiancé."

Caroline paced back and forth anxiously as the prelude music to the wedding continued in the distance. She shook her head in mute disapproval. "I am sure Patrice already knew." And more, was completely okay with it!

"Well, then—" Sela motioned for the guitars to keep playing, regardless of how long it took to get the actual ceremony under way "—what difference does it make?"

Caroline looked over at the three hundred wedding guests assembled on the lawn, alternately chatting among themselves and looking for the first signs of the wedding party. Caroline frowned. "Have you not noticed how restless the guests are getting?" She couldn't help but note that the reporter and photographer from *Fort Worth* magazine were looking at the motor homes, too. And probably, Caroline worried, speculating about the reason behind the delay. None of this was good! "The ceremony should have started fifteen minutes ago!" Caroline fumed.

Looking as pulled together as always in a vibrant red-and-gold dress that fit perfectly with the Cinco de Mayo theme, Sela pronounced seriously, "I think the guests will live, despite the delay."

Sela came closer, studying the expression on Caroline's face. "Seriously, why is this so upsetting to you? And don't tell me it's the potential damage to your professional reputation, because I don't buy that for one second. At no time have you ever put your own needs above those of the client. So why are you taking this so personally? Why do you feel that Jack has let *you* down—when he's only doing what he feels he has to do?"

Usually Caroline appreciated Sela's concern, but today it was only aggravating. "He went behind his mother's back to investigate Dutch!" Just as Caroline's ex-fiancé had meddled behind hers! Caroline continued miserably. "He's been trying to manage Patrice's life for her, without her knowledge or consent."

"He was trying to protect her. For all Jack knew, in the end he'd have nothing to tell Patrice. I'm sure that was what he was hoping would happen, anyway."

Caroline couldn't deny that.

"And frankly," Sela asserted, "if it were my children, and they thought I wasn't seeing something clearly and was about to make a huge life-altering mistake, I'd want them to intervene on my behalf, too."

"Even if they turned out to be wrong in the end?" Caroline asked, rubbing at the tense muscles in the back of her neck. She didn't know when she had ever felt so depressed and dejected.

"Yes." Sela leaned toward Caroline, determined to make her point. "And you know why? Because their actions, however misguided, would show me that they love me and that they were willing to follow their convictions, even at the risk I would be angry with them. And they would dare that because they know I love them and would forgive them any frailty."

Guilt mixed with the resentment deep inside her. "It's not that easy, not anymore," Caroline mumbled.

Jack had never come right out and said he loved her, but he had certainly made her feel as if he did! And that had given her the confidence to wish for all the things that she wanted. A good man to love, who would love her back. A little girl to mother. A mom to replace the one she'd lost, the father figure she'd never had. She'd even had an adorable trouble-prone golden retriever to liven up her life! Being part of Jack's life was the closest she had ever gotten to living the American Dream.

The only problem was, her joy had been based on an expectation that could not last.

Slowly, Caroline released the breath she had been holding and revealed what was in her heart. "It was all so easy, Sela. Falling for Jack, getting to know and love his family, becoming part of his world." The ache in Caroline's throat matched the pain in her heart as she reluctantly confessed, "I thought my dreams had finally been realized, that Jack and I had the perfect relationship, the kind that would endure any difficulty that could possibly come our way. Instead, the first real crisis that came along tore us apart and forced me to acknowledge that while the pursuit of happiness is everything to me, it is nothing to Jack. His heart is so guarded, his faith of achieving any kind of ongoing personal fulfillment so low, he's never going to let me in his life and his heart, not the way I need. It's going to be his way or nothing at all. And he just expects me to stay silent and understand."

Sela frowned. "I'm not sure that's true."

"He knew how important it was to me to give his mother and Dutch the blissfully happy wedding day they deserve," Caroline declared. Especially given the fact that Dutch was ill! She pointed to the luxury motor home where Jack, Dutch and Patrice were still sequestered. "And he's in there right now trying to derail it anyway."

"On the strength of his convictions, which in this case do not match yours," Sela countered with sensitivity and understanding. "Look at it this way. You and I work very hard to create the weddings of people's dreams. But no matter how hard we try, there is always some glitch. Sometimes it's big—like that tornado that touched down just west of here on Friday. Other times it's a little thing, like a box of silverware that went astray. But you and I accept that as part of the job, part of life. The same thing goes for our humanity. Jack is not without flaws. And neither are you. The dream man you are searching for does not exist and you need to think about that before you give up on Jack entirely."

Caroline pushed aside the suspicion that she was being way too unrealistic in her goals, as a way of protecting her own heart. "What are you saying?" she asked uneasily.

Sela looked her in the eye. "Simply that maybe in this case it's not Jack you should be looking to change."

CAROLINE THOUGHT ABOUT what Sela said during the moments before Dutch and Patrice emerged from the motor home, while Jack escorted his mother down the aisle, and as the happy couple said their vows.

By the time the buffet dinner was served, she knew what she had to do. The only problem was, there were still many wedding festivities left to oversee. So Caroline did her job. She kept the buffet tables filled with all sorts of Tex-Mex specialties. Reassured Jericho nothing untoward was going to happen to the cake. And maintained a vigil over Bounder, who was happily off leash and laying next to Maddie's chair at the kid table.

To her disappointment, Jack didn't make any attempt to speak to her. Nor was there any indication of whether or not he planned to forgive her. He simply seemed…pensive, too.

Caroline tried not to think what that might mean.

Or worry about the warm spring breeze that seemed to get a little stronger and a little gustier with every minute that passed.

Late afternoon, the skies were still clear.

Which meant the dancing could commence unobstructed on the outdoor dance floor as soon as the toasts were over.

The microphones were turned on and the best man went first, followed by the maid of honor. Several other friends and members of the wedding party jumped in to have their say. Finally, Jack raised his glass and stood. The sudden emotion on his face as he looked to the crowd and then the happy couple brought a lump to Caroline's throat.

"Courage comes in all forms. Daring to fall in love—" Jack paused to lift his glass to Dutch and Patrice "—is certainly at the top of the list." His mother smiled as she met his eyes. "Taking on the planning of a huge wedding and making it a dream come true, in just three weeks—" this time Jack paused and held Caroline's gaze in a way that set her heart pounding "—is certainly another. And then," Jack continued, grinning mischievously, "there's agreeing to include a mostly well-behaved family pet in the nuptials."

Everyone laughed. Bounder had been a total ham as she trotted down the aisle, tail up, flowers spilling out of the cloth basket strapped to her back, a beaming, prancing Maddie tossing blossoms at her side.

"And then there's a truly remarkable form of courage," Jack said, his voice sounding a little hoarse. "The type that only the most selfless of us can claim. It's the kind of courage that has us putting the needs of others ahead of our own. The recognition that life can change in an instant. Sometimes in ways we expect. Other times in a way that is a total surprise. What I'm trying to say…is that love is the only thing that really matters in this world. When you find it, I advise you to hold on to it with all you've got." Jack stopped again and looked straight at Caroline, before turning once again to the happy couple at the bride and groom's table. "The way Dutch and my mom have.

I advise you to follow their example and focus on living every moment to the very fullest. Because all any of us really have for certain, is today. And today—" Jack's voice caught "—Dutch and Patrice are together. They are here as man and wife, bravely showing us what it is to risk all for the love of another." Caroline couldn't be sure, but she thought she saw tears glistening in Jack's eyes as he finished, more emotionally than ever. "So let's raise our glasses in toast, and wish the happy couple the love and happiness they have earned."

"YOU CAN STOP beaming now," Sela whispered in Caroline's ear.

"I can't help it," Caroline whispered back, feeling a little overcome with emotion herself. She was about to burst into happy tears as a gust of wind blew through the tent, ruffling the hems of tablecloths, threatening for one tense moment to upset the cake. Luckily, Jericho was right there to steady the table it was standing on. And the near-catastrophe was enough of a momentary distraction to allow Caroline to pull herself together. Caroline swallowed and continued in a low, even voice. "Jack did himself proud just now."

"And you, from the looks of it, given the way you obviously helped get through to him," Sela teased.

Caroline grinned as another gust of wind swept over the flat, Texas plains, billowing through the tent and whipping up the hems of the tablecloths. Glasses rattled, a few were tossed onto their sides. Champagne spilled, and behind the bride and groom the wedding piñata swung back and forth in a way all too reminiscent of the "leaping deer" it was purported to be. And yet Caroline remained wildly optimistic about the way the rest of the evening would go.

If Jack could change his mind about Dutch and Patrice's marriage, surely he could find it in his heart to forgive her? At least, Caroline thought, as she quickly moved to secure the wildly swaying piñata, she hoped that was the case.

"Caroline!" Maddie stopped her en route.

Figuring the piñata could wait—this was definitely more important—Caroline knelt down to hug the little girl. Maddie hugged Caroline back just as warmly, then stated happily, "Bounder and I both want to dance with you tonight!"

That was an interesting prospect, Maddie thought, her spirits rising even more.

"Can we?" Maddie persisted.

Caroline envisioned first Maddie standing on her toes as they swayed to the music, then Bounder, or perhaps both of them at the same time, a dog on her right foot, a little girl on her left. Caroline laughed at the mental image, knowing one way or another they'd figure it out. "Sure."

"Because you know, next time it will be your time to be the bride," Maddie said. "And we've got to practice!"

Caroline flushed. Much as she might dream it, *that* was getting a little ahead of the game.

Before she could formulate a suitable comeback, however, a third gust of wind swept through the enormous white dinner tent, this one rattling the ceiling of the tent and the poles suspending it, too.

Caroline looked over to see the wedding piñata swinging wildly. She gasped in dismay. Maddie pointed. And Bounder, good dog that she was, leaped up to save the day.

IT WASN'T A RABBIT, JACK thought, but it may as well have been one, for all the havoc it caused.

Bounder jumped to her feet and to the shocked laughter

of the guests, raced between the maze of round tables to the long rectangular one that housed the wedding party. Sizing up the situation and "the threat" of her quarry in a millisecond, Bounder reared back on two paws. She leaped with a prima ballerina's grace, flying through the air and easily clearing the "hurdle" of bride and groom. Still suspended in midair, the golden retriever grabbed the swaying white piñata between her jaws and landed spryly on the ground once more. New gasps of dismay turned to gales of laughter as the dog took off through the opening in the dining tent, taking the candy-filled "deer" along with her.

Caroline was right after Bounder, in hot pursuit.

Waving for everyone else to stay back, Jack ran after Caroline.

His heart racing, he followed the two of them between the rows of chairs where the ceremony had taken place, through another field of brilliantly colored wildflowers, and then back again, to the flower-laced wedding arbor.

Only there, in the safety of the covered haven, partially shielded from the blowing wind, did Bounder finally sink down, the piñata still in her jaws.

"Bounder, no!" Caroline cried, sinking down beside her.

Too late, Jack noted. The side of the piñata had been ripped open.

"It's chocolate!" Caroline shouted as Jack reached them, too.

And Bounder could not have chocolate, Jack knew.

Jack reached down and put a hand over Bounder's snout. "Bounder, no," he told the golden retriever firmly. "That's poisonous. Chocolate can kill a dog. You have to let go. *Now*, Bounder."

But Bounder, it seemed, didn't care what the master

ordered. She wasn't budging. She lay, the piñata trapped between her two front paws, and clenched firmly in her jaws.

But at least, Jack thought, sinking down to the grass, too, Bounder wasn't ingesting any of the candy. And indeed, the golden seemed to have given up the idea of further tearing the deer apart, as long as she could lay there, triumphant in the victory of having saved the wedding party from the "danger" of the wildly swinging piñata.

Caroline looked over at Jack.

Still breathing hard, as out of breath as he, she looked... incredible.

Like all the guests there, Jack noted, Caroline had dressed in clothing appropriate for a "Fifth of May" festival of love, marriage and life.

In her case, that meant an off-the-shoulder white blouse that bared all of her shoulders and most of her arms, and a full rainbow-striped skirt that swung out from her hips in an increasingly wide swirl, ending just below the knee. Her feet were clad in stack-heeled espadrilles that were as sexy as they were practical. She wore no jewelry except for a heart-shaped pendant that swung against her breasts and a pair of hoop earrings. Her copper hair was deliciously tousled. Her cheeks pink from exertion. Her eyes were the same brilliant blue of the wildflowers in the fields all around them. She looked beautiful and vulnerable and strong, and he was more taken with her than ever.

Abruptly, Caroline grinned. Her eyes twinkled. "We have got to stop meeting like this," she said.

OKAY, CAROLINE THOUGHT, maybe she shouldn't have made a joke, given the way they had left things between them a few hours ago.

Maybe she should have started with an apology. Or

a heartfelt declaration of love. Or an outright plea for forgiveness.

But as far as Jack was concerned, judging by the sparkle in his eyes, she had done it exactly right.

"Actually..." Jack reached out and took her hand. His eyes darkened with sensual intent. "I think this is exactly how we should meet." The raw emotion in his voice caused a riptide of feeling in her. He looked over at her, his expression somber. "That is, if you can find it in your heart to forgive me. You were right all along." His callused palm gripped hers. "I should have stayed out of it, let my mother make her own decisions."

She looked into his silver-gray eyes, knowing this was all-important if they were ever to be truly happy together. "Why didn't you?" she asked softly. She needed reassurance that their life together wouldn't be hampered by endless conditions and restrictions. That it would be the joint partnership they both needed and deserved.

He regarded her soberly and she saw the love she felt for him reflected back. "Because it was easier to worry about someone else than to contemplate how afraid I've been ever since my dad was taken ill, to commit myself to anything other than the present."

"But you married, built a business, had a child...." Caroline looked down at Bounder, who was now resting her cheek on her "prize." With her free hand, she petted the dog's soft blond head. "You bought a home and got a completely lovable, slightly trouble-prone pup...." Who was as determined as her seven-year-old mistress, it seemed, to bring her and Jack together.

Jack chuckled at the joke and flashed Caroline a crooked smile. "There's no doubt I thought I was doing fine," he admitted, shifting position and drawing Caroline closer still. "Until you came along and showed me I wasn't. I love my family and our dog, my friends. I would do anything for them. But in the process of holding on to all that, and making sure I didn't lose anything that I had the way I'd lost my father, I forgot what it was to hold a dream in my heart. To give myself over to something, or in this case someone—" he paused and looked deep into her eyes "—so completely that I would risk everything."

A thrill swept through her. A smidgen of hope grew deep inside her. "And now you do know how to do that?"

He nodded, all the affection she had ever wanted to see on his face. "I love you, Caroline." He wrapped both his arms around her. "With all my heart and soul."

Caroline wreathed both her arms around his neck. "Oh, Jack," she whispered, reveling in the words she had so wanted to hear. "I love you, too." She kissed him deeply, tenderly. "So much it scared me. Which is why I made the classic mistake a lot of brides make."

Jack lifted a quizzical brow.

Luxuriating in the comfort of his warm embrace and the potent resolve on his face, she explained, "Lusting after perfection in a relationship might be admirable, but it's not practical or advisable. Real life is full of unforeseen complications, unexpected events and hard decisions. To think you and I would agree on everything is ridiculous. But I kept telling myself that I couldn't be with anyone who didn't see things exactly as I saw them all the time, because it was easier than putting myself out there again and risking my heart, the way I have risked it with you from the very first moment we met. Which is why—" Caroline took a deep breath and took that giant leap of faith "—I'm about to do something I never thought I would do." She opened her heart to him all the way, gazed deep into his eyes, and made the proposal of a lifetime. "I want us to be together, the way we were meant to be. And make each other's dreams come true."

# *Epilogue*

*One year later...*

"Is this going to be all ours, Mommy?" Maddie asked.

Caroline smiled over at her newly adopted eight-year-old daughter and the beloved family pet that was always at Maddie's side. Caroline hugged Maddie, then reached down to pet Bounder behind her ears. The golden retriever wagged her tail so ecstatically, she nearly fell over. Maddie giggled and her daddy chuckled. Grinning, too, Caroline turned to look at Jack. Appreciating how handsome he looked, anytime, anywhere, as well as how loved her new husband made her feel, she slipped her hand in his. "What do you think?" she asked him.

Jack studied the ocean from the beach house deck. "It's definitely a spectacular view of the Gulf," he murmured, unable to help but be impressed with the five-thousand-square-foot, three-story, hurricane-proof residence on the stretch of private sand.

Together, they all turned back to look at Dutch and Patrice. "But it's a little much, don't you think, for a wedding present?"

Looking every bit as healthy, happy and content as they all could have wished, Dutch and Patrice shook their heads.

"We want you to have a place of your own to stay whenever you come visit," Dutch said.

Patrice smiled and slipped her arm around Dutch's waist. "All you have to do is say yes."

Caroline laughed softly and squeezed Jack's hand. "We seem to be doing a lot of that lately." And all to good result.

Together, they'd said yes to six months of dating, followed by a six-month engagement and marriage. Caroline had adopted Maddie. And agreed to an addition to the family, in the form of a new puppy and a "little sister" for Bounder.

Patrice was enjoying married life so much she'd been asked to create a new fragrance for "Seniors in Love" for Couture Perfume.

Dutch had been accepted into the clinical trial and the new drug they were testing was indeed a miracle. His kidney disease had been halted in its tracks, the damage to his kidneys reversed. Consequently, Dutch had been taken off dialysis and the transplant list, and was in fact feeling so good these days that he had decided to keep his beachfront properties on South Padre Island, and go back to managing them himself.

Jack had more business than he could handle.

And thanks to the glowing reviews of Patrice and Dutch's memorable Cinco de Mayo–themed wedding in *Fort Worth* magazine, Caroline had become, just as she wanted, The Hot New Wedding Planner to Hire in both Dallas and Fort Worth. Her former assistant now had a full client list of her own, and Jericho had become the hottest wedding cake designer in the Metroplex.

"So what do you say?" Dutch asked them. "Does this look like it might be a good second home for you—all? A place to come and unwind?"

"It looks like the perfect place," Jack said. He shook hands with the stepfather he had come to know and love. "Thank you."

"We really appreciate your generosity," Caroline said.

Jack turned back to Caroline. He looked her in the eye. She knew what he was thinking. It was the same thing she was thinking.

"Shall we tell them?" he asked.

Without warning, tears of sheer happiness were misting her eyes. Caroline nodded. "Absolutely," she said in a choked voice.

"I knew it!" Patrice clapped her hands, ecstatic.

"Knew what?" Maddie piped up, perplexed.

Dutch surveyed them all sagely. "I think we're getting another new addition to the family," Dutch said.

Maddie's brows furrowed in consternation. "We can't have more than one new puppy at a time, Daddy said."

Jack knelt in front of his daughter. "Then how about a new baby instead?" he asked Maddie gently.

Maddie had to think about that for a second. "Is it going to be a brother or a sister?" she asked.

Caroline and Jack grinned. "We don't know yet."

"That's okay." Maddie wrinkled her nose. "Because I like both. And this way, I won't have to decide which one I want." Maddie hugged Jack, then launched herself into Caroline's waiting arms and held on tight. She tipped her head back and looked up at Caroline adoringly. "We'll just be surprised and all find out together. Won't we, Mommy?"

Her heart swelling with more love and contentment than she ever imagined she could feel, Caroline held her little girl close. "We sure will," she said thickly, as more hugs and congratulations were exchanged all around, then Patrice and Dutch took Maddie and Bounder down to explore the beach.

Once again, Jack and Caroline were alone.

He took her in his arms, stroked her hair, delivered a long, sweet, tender, soul-searching kiss. When at last they came up for air, he looked around once again and murmured, "I can imagine us being very happy here."

"So can I," Caroline whispered back. Smiling, she stood on tiptoe and kissed him again. At last, they all had everything they ever wanted. Life was good indeed.

\* \* \* \* \*

*There's one more single man in this group of friends!*
*Watch for Nate's story*
*THE MOMMY PROPOSAL*
*Coming August 2010*
*Only from Harlequin American Romance!*

*Harlequin offers a romance for every mood!*
*See below for a sneak peek*
*from our paranormal romance line,*
*Silhouette® Nocturne™.*
*Enjoy a preview of REUNION by USA TODAY*
*bestselling author Lindsay McKenna.*

Aella closed her eyes and sensed a distinct shift, like movement from the world around her to the unseen world.

She opened her eyes. And had a slight shock at the man standing ten feet away. He wasn't just any man. Her heart leaped and pounded. He reminded her of a fierce warrior from an ancient civilization. Incan? She wasn't sure but she felt his deep power and masculinity.

*I'm Aella. Are you the guardian of this sacred site?* she asked, hoping her telepathy was strong.

Fox's entire body soared with joy. Fox struggled to put his personal pleasure aside.

*Greetings, Aella. I'm the assistant guardian to this sacred area. You may call me Fox. How can I be of service to you, Aella?* he asked.

*I'm searching for a green sphere. A legend says that the Emperor Pachacuti had seven emerald spheres created for the Emerald Key necklace. He had seven of his priestesses and priests travel the world to hide these spheres from evil forces. It is said that when all seven spheres are found, restrung and worn, that Light will return to the Earth. The fourth sphere is here, at your sacred site. Are you aware of it?* Aella held her breath. She loved looking at him, especially his sensual mouth. The desire to kiss him came out of nowhere.

Fox was stunned by the request. *I know of the Emerald Key necklace because I served the emperor at the time it was created. However, I did not realize that one of the spheres is here.*

Aella felt sad. Why? Every time she looked at Fox, her heart felt as if it would tear out of her chest. *May I stay in touch with you as I work with this site?* she asked.

*Of course.* Fox wanted nothing more than to be here with her. To absorb her ephemeral beauty and hear her speak once more.

Aella's spirit lifted. What *was* this strange connection between them? Her curiosity was strong, but she had more pressing matters. In the next few days, Aella knew her life would change forever. How, she had no idea....

*Look for REUNION*
*by USA TODAY bestselling author Lindsay McKenna*
*Available April 2010*
*Only from Silhouette® Nocturne™*

## HARLEQUIN Romance®

## ROMANCE, RIVALRY AND A FAMILY REUNITED

THE BRIDES *of* BELLA ROSA

William Valentine and his beloved wife, Lucia, live
a beautiful life together, but when his former love Rosa
and the secret family they had together resurface,
an instant rivalry is formed. Can these families
get through the past and come together as one?

---

*Step into the world of Bella Rosa
beginning this April with*

# Beauty and the Reclusive Prince
### *by*
# RAYE MORGAN

*Eight volumes to collect and treasure!*

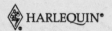

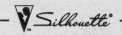

# SPECIAL EDITION

INTRODUCING A BRAND-NEW MINISERIES
FROM *USA TODAY* BESTSELLING AUTHOR

# KASEY MICHAELS

## SECOND-CHANCE BRIDAL

At twenty-eight, widowed single mother
Elizabeth Carstairs thinks she's left love behind
forever....until she meets Will Hollingsbrook.
Her sons' new baseball coach is the handsomest
man she's ever seen—and the more time they
spend together, the more undeniable the
connection between them. But can Elizabeth
leave the past behind and open her heart to
a second chance at love?

### FIND OUT IN

# SUDDENLY A BRIDE

*Available in April
wherever books are sold.*

**Visit Silhouette Books at www.eHarlequin.com**

SSE65517

# HER MEDITERRANEAN PLAYBOY

*Sexy and dangerous—he wants you in his bed!*

The sky is blue, the azure sea is crashing against the golden sand and the sun is hot.

The conditions are perfect for a scorching Mediterranean seduction from two irresistible untamed playboys!

*Indulge your senses with these two delicious stories*

## A MISTRESS AT THE ITALIAN'S COMMAND
*by Melanie Milburne*

## ITALIAN BOSS, HOUSEKEEPER MISTRESS
*by Kate Hewitt*

Available April 2010 from Harlequin Presents!

www.eHarlequin.com

HP12910

# REQUEST YOUR FREE BOOKS!
## 2 FREE NOVELS PLUS 2 FREE GIFTS!

HARLEQUIN®

*American ★ Romance®*

### Love, Home & Happiness!

**YES!** Please send me 2 FREE Harlequin® American Romance® novels and my 2 FREE gifts (gifts are worth about $10). After receiving them, if I don't wish to receive any more books, I can return the shipping statement marked "cancel." If I don't cancel, I will receive 4 brand-new novels every month and be billed just $4.24 per book in the U.S. or $4.99 per book in Canada. That's a saving of close to 15% off the cover price! It's quite a bargain! Shipping and handling is just 50¢ per book in the U.S. and 75¢ per book in Canada.* I understand that accepting the 2 free books and gifts places me under no obligation to buy anything. I can always return a shipment and cancel at any time. Even if I never buy another book from Harlequin, the two free books and gifts are mine to keep forever.

154 HDN E4CC   354 HDN E4CN

| | | |
|---|---|---|
| Name | (PLEASE PRINT) | |
| Address | | Apt. # |
| City | State/Prov. | Zip/Postal Code |

Signature (if under 18, a parent or guardian must sign)

#### Mail to the **Harlequin Reader Service:**
**IN U.S.A.:** P.O. Box 1867, Buffalo, NY 14240-1867
**IN CANADA:** P.O. Box 609, Fort Erie, Ontario L2A 5X3

Not valid for current subscribers to Harlequin® American Romance® books.

**Want to try two free books from another line?**
Call 1-800-873-8635 or visit www.morefreebooks.com.

\* Terms and prices subject to change without notice. Prices do not include applicable taxes. N.Y. residents add applicable sales tax. Canadian residents will be charged applicable provincial taxes and GST. Offer not valid in Quebec. This offer is limited to one order per household. All orders subject to approval. Credit or debit balances in a customer's account(s) may be offset by any other outstanding balance owed by or to the customer. Please allow 4 to 6 weeks for delivery. Offer available while quantities last.

**Your Privacy:** Harlequin is committed to protecting your privacy. Our Privacy Policy is available online at www.eHarlequin.com or upon request from the Reader Service. From time to time we make our lists of customers available to reputable third parties who may have a product or service of interest to you. If you would prefer we not share your name and address, please check here. ☐

**Help us get it right**—We strive for accurate, respectful and relevant communications. To clarify or modify your communication preferences, visit us at www.ReaderService.com/consumerschoice.

HAR10